SLOCUM A TRAITOR?

One of the troopers fired a shot, the bullet narrowly missing Slocum and ricocheting off the boulder behind him before whining away and slamming into the canyon wall.

Slocum took another step forward, and then a third. "Warren, listen to me! Put down your guns. No one is going to hurt you."

He walked toward Anderson's horse, keeping his hands high so that the troopers could see him.

"Gone over to the other side, have you, Slocum?" Anderson snapped.

SPECIAL PREVIEW!

Turn to the back of this book for an exciting excerpt from the magnificent new series . . .

RAILS WEST!

. . . the grand and epic story of the West's first railroads—and the brave men and women who forged an American dream.

Available from Jove Books

JAKE LOGAN

POWDER RIVER MASSACRE

BERKLEY BOOKS, NEW YORK

POWDER RIVER MASSACRE

A Berkley Book / published by arrangement with
the author

PRINTING HISTORY
Berkley edition / May 1993

ISBN: 0-425-13665-5

A BERKLEY BOOK ® TM 757,375
Berkley Books are published by The Berkley Publishing Group,
200 Madison Avenue, New York, New York 10016.
The name "BERKLEY" and the "B" logo
are trademarks belonging to Berkley Publishing Corporation.

PRINTED IN THE UNITED STATES OF AMERICA

10 9 8 7 6 5 4 3 2 1

1

The smoke spiraled up toward the heavens, twisting and writhing like a serpent in its death throes. High above, it seemed to disappear as it was torn apart by the winds, becoming wisps too small and transparent to be seen. It was still there, the man watching knew, and what troubled him was not where it went, but where it had come from.

John Slocum dug the rowels deep into the flanks of his big roan, then used the reins to lash a little more speed out of the game stallion. The Powder River country was no place to be for a white man on his own, not with bands of Sioux roaming the lush valleys hunting for bear, and ready to lift any pale-skinned scalp they happened across.

No stranger to danger, Slocum was less worried about marauding bands of Sioux warriors than he was about his job. He had just started the week before, and he needed the money. It seemed strange to have someone pay him to defend a railroad that hadn't even been built yet, but as long as the pay was there at the end of the month, he'd do the work.

The Northern Pacific Railroad had been struggling across the northern plains for a few years now, and the Sioux were only one of a legion of troubles that seemed to plague it at every turn. The financial panic of 1873 had driven more than one of the railroad's investors into bankruptcy, and sent a few diving out of tenth-story windows onto the pavements of New York City and Chicago.

Those investors who managed to get through the panic with their holdings intact had found themselves confronted by a welter of land disputes, labor troubles, suits, and countersuits. From what Slocum had heard, the lawyers back east must have been studying Quantrill's tactics: hit and run, slash and burn, feint and withdraw—but most of all, take no prisoners.

It was a wonder any of the investors got any sleep or had two dimes to rub together. John Slocum was no stranger to frontier guerilla thinking or to the greed that seemed to slumber like a hibernating bear just under the heart of every friend and neighbor.

He'd done his part in the Late War, and came home to find everything he'd fought for either dead and buried, like his family, or, like the Slocum family holdings, in the hands of people he'd known all his life, like the men who had played poker with his father on summer Sunday afternoons.

That was water under the bridge now. For most men, that would have been enough. But John Slocum was not most men. Water or not, he had ridden across the bridge, taken a torch to it, and never looked back. Georgia was two thousand miles and a dozen lifetimes ago now. It was still there in his memory, like the phantom pain of an amputated limb, or a faint scar that no one ever mentioned, but you could not fail to see whenever you came within shouting distance of a mirror. Knowing it was there was enough to make it hurt, even now, more than a little.

But all of that was in the past. Today was full of smoke, smoke of an unknown origin, the source of which he could only guess at, and while guessing, whisper a little prayer and hope that he was wrong. More often than not, such prayers went unanswered. As the roan galloped toward the thick column of black smoke, he knew that this one would likely go unfulfilled.

The plains were deceiving, and the distance could tease you again and again. Every rise seemed to be the last between a man and his destination. Cresting one would only reveal another, and then another, and on they would go, teasing him mile after mile, until he swore than he would turn his back and ride away rather than be disappointed one more time. Sometimes, men came to believe that they were seeing nothing more than an illusion, chasing an image every bit as deceptive and tantalizing as the distant glimpse of green that duped a man dying of thirst in the desert.

But the smoke was all too real, and Slocum hoped that his worst fears as to what he would find at the base of the churning black column would not be realized. He kept lashing the roan, urging it on faster and faster. He knew that the Sioux covered vast distances by walking their horses up a hill and running them full tilt down the far side, letting them conserve their energy for the serious business that invariably waited at the end of a long ride.

But Slocum didn't have that luxury. A supply wagon was overdue, a day late, and probably in trouble. The survey team's camp, far out in front of the main construction camp, was running low on food and ammunition, and there wasn't a man in the camp who didn't think the teamsters had run afoul of a war party.

In the valley ahead of him, a broad creek wound its way through hip-deep grass. Willows and cottonwoods shielded much of the watercourse from view, but here and there he caught the glint of sunlight on the placid surface. Blades of light slashed up through the willow branches, flickering as a slight breeze caused the limbs to sway gently.

On the far side of the creek, the base of the column of smoke was hidden from view, and he knew it wouldn't be a pleasant sight when he reached its source. Already, the smoke was beginning to abate, the column now wavering as the blaze beneath it had begun to die. Slocum pushed the roan downhill at a breakneck pace, the big horse galloping easily through the grass as its rider angled across the slope, heading for a break in the trees.

Slowing as he reached the brush that fanned out away from the creek on both sides, he let the horse walk through the tangled scrub, then step gingerly onto the sandy bank and down into the water. The creek wasn't very deep, and was about twenty yards wide. Its surface rippled around an occasional rock, and the water burbled softly. The sibilant splashes of the roan's hooves drowned out the steady murmuring until the horse climbed out of the creek on the far side.

Slocum caught sight of a trout darting toward a fly drifting on the surface. The trout nabbed the fly, then, with a flick of its tail, vanished into deeper water behind a large, flat rock. It would have been altogether a peaceful scene had it not been for what he suspected lay on the other side of the screen of undergrowth.

The roan shouldered its way through the brush and out into the tall grass, and there it was—a wagon bed, the arching hoops of steel to support its canvas cover charred black. Thick smoke still billowed around the hoops, and tongues of flame licked up along the sides of the wagon bed.

The bottom of the bed had burned through in a couple of places. Heaps of charred debris glowed beneath it, burning a dull orange that brightened to white, then faded to cherry red as the breeze rose and fell, breathing momentary life into the dying blaze.

One of the horses lay dead. The other, sprung from the traces, grazed serenely fifty yards away, as if it had no connection with the wreckage still smoldering behind it.

Slocum dismounted, and scanned the ridge rising gently skyward on the far side of the wagon, looking for traces of who might have set the blaze. He let the roan walk behind him, keeping the reins looped once around his fingers, tangled in his fist.

Where were the teamsters, he wondered, and why was there no sign of life, other than the solitary horse?

Covering the two hundred yards between the brush and the burning wagon with caution, he kept his gaze darting from the wreckage to the ridge line and back. Nothing moved except the switching tail of the single horse.

The wagon was familiar. As he drew closer, he saw the stenciled letters NPRR outlined against the blackened side of the wagon. Scorched and faded by the flames, they were a sheen of ghostly silver, more shadow than anything else.

"Hello? Anyone there?"

No one answered Slocum's call. But then again, he hadn't really expected an answer. He took another few steps, then stopped in his tracks. The breeze glided across the grass, bending the blades and sending a ripple of silver up the slope. He watched the retreating wave until it sank into motionlessness, the way a circle generated by a stone will slowly drift across the surface of a lake and vanish; swallowed up by the water through which it moved.

Once more, he called out, "Hello? Anybody here?"

And again, he got no answer.

Tugging on the reins, he started to run, pulling the roan along behind him. He could hear the hiss of the grass against his legs, and the muffled thudding of the roan's hooves on the turf. A crack startled him as he saw the side of the wagon fall to the ground, sending up a shower of sparks and a swirl of whitish smoke. Another crack, and then the rear axle broke. The left rear wheel fell over and the weight of the wagon collapsed behind it.

That was when he saw the man.

Flat on his back, charred almost beyond recognition, the man had his arms curled around his head as if trying to ward off a blow from an unseen fist. Slocum let go of the reins and sprinted the last twenty yards to the wagon.

He could smell it now, the sickening stench of charred flesh, and the strong, almost choking smell of burned hair. He could see bone in places where the flesh had cooked and shriveled; the man's ribs looked gray under the remains of skin and muscle where they poked through.

The face was all but gone. The eyes had burst, and the sockets oozed a yellowish gore that looked more like bacon grease than anything human. It trailed down across the cheekbones and was smeared on the remains of the wagon bed where the body had shifted as the wagon fell.

On closer examination, the blackened stubs of wood protruding from the man's midsection were recognizable as the remains of two arrows. Slocum breathed a sigh of relief; the man must have been dead before the flames had consumed him. It looked like Johnny Carlson, but he couldn't be sure. He was barely certain that the blackened wreckage in front of him had been a human being at all.

Several arrows protruded from the other side of the wagon, which was less damaged by the fire. Their shafts were charred, but not enough to have destroyed the distinctive markings. *Sioux*, he thought.

But where was the other man? Where was Davey Chilton? It had been a two-man crew. The other body would be nearby somewhere. Slocum started to circle the wagon, looking in the tall grass. He was certain that if the second man had survived, he would not have gone off on foot, certainly not with the dray horse still healthy. He might have hidden until the attack was over, but still would not have risked trying to get back to the main camp on foot.

Around and around he went, gradually widening the circle. By his fourth pass, he still had found no sign of the missing man. On his fifth, warding off clouds of flies that swarmed up out of the grass, he found the first evidence. A smear of blood on the blades, not much, probably not a serious wound and almost certainly not fatal, he thought.

But where in hell was the wounded man?

"Hey, it's John Slocum," he called. "Davey? Davey Chilton, are you out there? Can you hear me?"

If he was, he still wasn't answering.

Slocum followed the trail of blood, and it was fairly easy; the passage of the wounded man had bent the grass, leaving a slight track, even though few of the blades had broken and most had already sprung back.

The path had started uphill, but then it curved back away from the wagon and back down toward the brush. That made sense; the dense thicket would have offered much better cover. Still, he was worried. If he could follow Chilton's progress this easily, so could the Sioux war party. That they hadn't bothered might mean that they had believed him dead, and weren't interested in a scalp. Or it could mean that something had frightened them off, but Slocum had no idea what that could have been.

Working his way back toward the trees, he followed the trail, still marked by faint smears of blood, into the brush and toward the water's edge. Stepping carefully into the brush, he wondered whether he was being set up. It was possible that the Sioux themselves had deliberately left the trail for him to follow—a little cheese in a mousetrap set just for him.

But he brushed the thought aside, pulled his Colt from its holster and entered the brush. He heard a groan then, somewhere ahead of him. Thumbing back the hammer on the Colt, he pushed aside the branches of a scrub oak in his path and leaned forward toward the edge of the creek. At first he saw nothing. Leaning farther forward, he thought he could see a patch of blue, possibly cloth, maybe Chilton's shirt.

Stepping into the clear, he saw a man lying on his side, one hand reaching for the water. The other was curled around the shaft of an arrow. A pool of blood had soaked into the sand beside him.

2

Slocum knelt by the wounded man. The arrow had passed through his side above the hip far enough for the arrowhead to pierce the skin of his back. Blood oozed out around it. Chilton was conscious, but just barely. Slocum gave him a twig to hold crosswise in his teeth.

"This is going to hurt a little, Davey, but we have to get that arrow out," he said.

Chilton groaned. "Just do it, Slocum," he said, his words barely intelligible as he bit down on the wood. The twig creaked a little, and Slocum thought for a moment Chilton was going to bite it clean through.

"Ready?"

The wounded man nodded. "Ready . . ."

Slocum looked at the arrowhead. The metal looked as if it had been hammered from a frying pan, which was common enough, but something about it caught his eye. The head was fitted parallel to the feathers at the other end of the shaft. This was the way hunting arrows were made. War arrows were made with the head perpendicular to the feathers. This enabled them to slide more easily between ribs, and penetrate more deeply and do more damage. No Sioux worth his salt went on a war party with a quiver full of hunting arrows.

He wondered about it, and the teamster noticed his hesitation. Removing the twig, Chilton gritted his teeth. "What the hell are you waiting for, man?" he said. "Get that damn thing out of me, will you?"

Slocum nodded. "All right, Davey, relax, will you? Just bite down on the stick." With his knife, Slocum cut partway through the shaft. The pressure made the man squirm. Every movement of the arrow was like a knife in Chilton's guts, and he moaned as he tried to control the pain.

Notching it enough to snap it cleanly, Slocum grasped the protruding end on either side of the cut. "Here goes nothing," he said.

He squeezed, and Chilton let out a yelp. The twig fell from between his teeth as his mouth opened. The arrow shaft snapped with a loud crack, and Chilton passed out cold as one last wave of pain rolled over him.

Slocum tucked the arrowhead into his pocket, then, taking advantage of the man's loss of consciousness, gripped the remainder of the shaft just below the feathers and jerked it free. There was a lot of blood, which he'd expected, but there was no other choice. He couldn't leave the arrow in for the long ride back to the survey camp.

Using strips torn from Chilton's shirt, he made two pads, one for the entrance wound and one for the exit wound. Then he knotted several of the strips together and tied the pads in place, while holding the wounded man in a sitting position until the makeshift bandages were secure.

That was the easy part, he thought. Now all I have to do is get him onto a horse and back to camp.

Getting to his feet, Slocum walked over to the dray horse, grabbed its bridle, and walked the skittish animal back to the creek bank. Removing the traces, he fashioned a network from the stiff leather. From his own mount, he took his bedroll, opened the blanket, folded it into a thick pad, and draped it over the horse's back. Then Slocum hoisted the unconscious teamster onto the horse. Without a saddle, Chilton had to be trussed up as if he were a prospector's pack. Using what was left of the traces, Slocum lashed the man to the animal's back, then used his rope to finish the job. It was a long ride, and he knew that the arrow wound needed medical attention. There was a surgeon with the survey crew, and the sooner Slocum got his man there, the better his chances of survival.

Looking at the remains of the wagon one more time, he shook his head. Something about the scene didn't seem right, but he didn't know why. He couldn't put his finger on the false note, but he was half-convinced there was more to the attack than met the eye.

Shaking off the momentary indecision, he swung into the saddle, and eased the roan close to the four-legged ambulance to get the tether rope. The dray horse was going to slow him down more than a little, and he whispered a silent prayer that he didn't run into the Sioux war party, if that's what it was, before getting help. If he did, he'd wasted his time patching up the teamster, and his own life would be over in a flash.

Slocum eased the roan through the brush, making sure that the pack horse followed him through the gaps in the undergrowth. Draped over the pack horse, the wounded Chilton was scraped and scratched by stiff branches, but there was nothing to be done about it. Easing into the water, Slocum started across the creek. The roan climbed out on the far side, bulled its way through the brush and out onto the grass.

Looking up the long slope with the grass waving in the

breeze, he could still see the path his descent had left behind, and headed straight for it. Working his way back up the slope, he set an easy pace. He wanted to hurry, but it was out of the question, and he knew he'd have to stop every couple of miles to make sure the bandages were holding. With the arrow removed, the bleeding might kill the teamster before he could reach help.

At the top of the ridge, he turned to look back at the valley floor. Plumes of thin smoke still drifted from the smoldering ruins of the wagon. He'd felt bad about not burying the dead man, but that would have to wait. A crew would come out the next day to take care of the burial. Lingering in the vicinity was an invitation to disaster. For all he knew, the Sioux might have been watching him all along, making plans to attack as soon as he was on the move.

He had field glasses in his saddlebags and decided to have a look. Opening the flap, he pulled out the scarred leather case, and raised the glasses to his eyes. Starting with the wagon, he swept the field glasses up the slope, then back down.

As near as he could tell, the opposite ridge was deserted. There was a chance, he knew, that the Sioux might have slipped around behind him while he tended to the wounded man. They might be lying in wait somewhere up ahead, but there was nothing he could do about that. He'd keep his eyes open and his Colt and Winchester handy.

Hanging the field glasses around his neck, he tucked their case back into the saddlebags and clucked to the roan. The valley ahead of him was a seamless sheet of green tinged with silver. As the wind rippled the grass, the blades twisted this way and that, their shiny surfaces catching the light and reflecting it back at him.

The only flaw that marred the huge green expanse was

the track of broken blades where he had passed through from the far end. Angling across the slope, he tugged the follow horse along in his wake, glancing back now and then to make sure that his freight was still securely lashed to the thick-legged chestnut.

As he neared the bottom of the hill, close to the narrow mouth of the valley, something caught his eye, and he swung around to look directly at it. At first, he couldn't find it, but he was certain that something had moved in the tall grass. For a moment, he conjured up a vision of a half-dozen warriors creeping toward him, using the grass as cover, but there were no streaks to betray any such presence. The Indians, he knew, were adept at parting the grass to permit passage without breaking a single blade, and then letting the grass spring back behind them. It was a precise skill requiring a delicacy which was at odds with the white man's view of the Indian as a brutal savage devoid of anything but a mindless dedication to brute force. But, in order to survive out here, it was a skill one had better learn.

Taking a deep breath and then letting it out in a soft whistle, he flapped his legs against the sides of the roan. As the horse started to move, he saw it again; this time he was sure that his eyes were not playing tricks on him. Bringing the glasses to bear, he trained them on the spot where he'd seen the movement.

Suddenly, a fawn darted out of the grass, rushed past him, and disappeared. Slocum sighed. Things were pretty bad when a small deer could make his heart stop beating. Shaking his head in embarrassment, he wondered how long it would have taken him to live it down, had anyone seen what had just happened.

He passed through the narrow mouth of the valley, glancing up at the steep, grass covered slopes on either side. Stunted oaks spilled down both sides of the valley mouth, and clumps of brush alternated with boulders in ragged lines. If the Sioux were going to hit him, they would have to look a long time to find a better place. The cover was almost perfect, and came so close to the valley floor that a hundred warriors could have been hidden among the rocks and brush without being seen.

He clucked to the roan, urging it to move faster. As he passed through, he kept his head swiveling from side to side, his eyes darting from nook to cranny, like bees zigzagging across a field of flowers. When he'd passed safely through into the next valley, he allowed himself to relax a little. "It's going to be a long day," he whispered.

As he rode, he debated whether to keep to the floor of the valley or stay higher up on the slope. There were advantages and disadvantages to either choice. High up the slope, he would be able to take cover on the far side of a ridge in a hurry. He could also see a greater distance, which was not an advantage to be taken lightly.

But the Sioux were fond of launching their attacks from concealment just out of sight behind a ridge. By staying far up the slope, he would be putting himself a whole lot closer to any war party lying in ambush, that is, if he guessed wrong, and happened to choose the ridge behind which the warriors waited.

If he stayed on the valley floor, he'd be farther away from a possible ambush, but his line of sight would be severely limited, and he would be susceptible to a quick encirclement as the warriors charged downhill at him. Any fool knew it was a lot easier for a man on horseback to go faster downhill than up.

The third option was, in some ways, the one with the biggest payoff but the highest risk. If he kept to the ridges, he could see for miles in any direction. This would enable him to spot approaching trouble long before it posed a genuine threat. But at the same time, he could be *seen* for miles, possibly calling unwanted attention to a passage that might otherwise have gone completely unnoticed.

There was no right answer, and there was no way to assess the relative odds. It was, he realized, a matter of pure chance. The best thing he could do was to make quick time to the survey camp and the security it offered. The crew and its guns would be a deterrent to small bands of Sioux, and with enough warning, could stand off an attack by as many as seventy-five or one hundred warriors.

Only one Sioux in four had firearms, if that many, and most of those guns were old. Some were even muzzle-loaders. They were chronically short on powder and their reloaded cartridges tended to be a little light. Slocum had heard more than one story about a man being struck with a bullet fired by a charging warrior and walking away with nothing more than a bad bruise to show for it.

The accuracy and long range of the Springfield and Winchester repeaters, and some Sharps carbines the army had been supplying in recent months, had allowed the military to fend off odds as high as ten to one, provided there had been cover available and enough ammunition. Of course, there was also the example of the Fetterman Massacre to serve as a cautionary reminder of the limits of firepower.

In some ways, the civilians were better armed than the army. Instead of the corruption that often accompanied negotiation of supply contracts, private corporations saw to it that their people were supplied with the best weapons money could buy. They were protecting potential fortunes, rather than making them in the process of buying and selling.

There was much about the white treatment of the Sioux that Slocum didn't like. Whenever he thought about it, which he tried not to do too often, he would realize that the Sioux were being exploited by friend and foe alike. He knew about the conditions on the reservations, where rotten corn, diseased cattle, and moldy flour were passed off as adequate supplies of food. At the same time, the dishonest Indian agents, and there were very few who weren't dishonest, were selling off some of the supplies to line their own pockets. To make more money still, the agents permitted the sale of whiskey to their charges, sometimes even selling it to the Sioux themselves.

But these were things about which Slocum could do nothing. And so, like many white men who disapproved of the way the red man was being treated, he pretended not to see.

It was the Sioux land that continued to draw white men west. The rolling country of the Powder River valley was ideal for raising horses and cattle. The Black Hills of Dakota Territory were full of gold, and the best routes to the far northwest for wagon and railroad alike, went through the heart of prime buffalo country.

There had been hundreds of victims, both red and white, of the relentless surge of civilization into Sioux territory. The latest such victim lay, little more than overcooked meat, in the bed of a burned-out wagon far behind him. And to prevent the man on the horse he led from becoming the next victim, Slocum had to get help in a hurry.

3

Slocum felt the eyes on his back. Rather than turn immediately, he rode on one hundred yards or so, then slowed. Trying not to let on that he was aware of anything out of the ordinary, he dismounted and walked back to the follow horse with a canteen dangling from one hand.

The teamster was groaning, but still seemed to be unconscious. Checking the bandages for bleeding, he realized that one of the pads had slipped. Davey's shirt was soaked with blood; a stain the size of a dinner plate was spreading down toward his hip and out over his rib cage.

It would be too risky to undo the ropes holding the wounded man on the horse, but he had to do something to impede the loss of blood. Tearing another piece of the cloth from the already-tattered work shirt, he wadded the scrap into a ball, folded it several times, then tucked it up under the pad.

Only when he'd finished with the bandage did he allow himself to look around. The hair on the back of his neck was standing straight up, like the ruff of an aroused terrier. Letting his gaze drift from one edge of the horizon to the other, he scanned the valley behind and below him.

There was no sign of anyone following him, but he knew, with a certainty that had nothing to do with the evidence of his eyes, that someone had been tailing him. The odds were it was one or more Sioux warriors, but there was nothing he could do about it, unless and until they showed themselves.

It would be suicide to attempt to confront them unless their intentions were rooted more in curiosity than hostile intent, a possibility which seemed too remote even to consider. No, if they were following him, they had a reason, and there was only one reason that made any sense.

He thought about making a flat out run for it, but the wounded man would never be able to take the jouncing and jostling a full gallop would subject him to. Slocum's only chance was to tough it out, swallow hard, climb back onto the roan, and ride on, as confident and serene as if he were the only man on the continent.

Unscrewing the cap of the canteen, he took a sip of the warm water, then tried to get Chilton to drink. Shaking him by the shoulder, he managed only to get a few moans out of him. The man's eyelids fluttered, and he turned his head trying to get a look at Slocum.

"Hurts like hell," he mumbled. "Where's my Ma? Want to talk to my Ma. . . ."

Nearly delirious, he lapsed back into unconsciousness. Slocum debated trying to wake him again, realizing that the bleeding had seriously dehydrated the wounded man. Slocum slapped his cheeks lightly, provoking another moan and an angry twist of the head.

When his eyes opened again, Slocum brought the canteen close. "Try to drink, Davey," he said. "You need to get some water into your body. Not too much, but a little."

The man shook his head, half in annoyance and half in confusion. "Not thirsty."

"Sure you are. You have to be, whether you know it or not. And you have to drink something."

"Not thirsty." He licked his lips, and his tongue scraped across the dry skin with a sound like parchment leaves being turned. "Not thirsty," he said again.

Slocum grabbed Chilton by the hair, turned his head sideways, and brought the canteen to his papery lips. Tilting it, he watched the man flick his tongue at the first few drops. When water started to trickle in a steady stream through his teeth, he allowed it collect, then tried to swallow, but he was unable to.

"Let the inside of your mouth loosen up a little, Davey," Slocum counseled. It'll be easier to swallow then."

Chilton nodded as if he understood what he had been told, and Slocum filled his mouth again. This time, the man swirled the water around, then swallowed.

"Better, Davey," Slocum said. "Now again." Once more, he tilted the canteen, filled the man's mouth and waited for him to swallow.

"More," Chilton said. "I'm so goddamned thirsty, Slocum. More."

Slocum shook his head. "Not now. I'll give you another drink in a little while. We have to get moving. I think we have company."

The man's eyes went wide. "What kind of company? You mean redskins?"

"Not sure. I think we're being followed. I don't know if we can get back to camp before sundown. If not, we're going to have a problem. You've lost quite a bit of blood already, and the surgeon will have to sew you up pretty soon, before you bleed to death."

"Didn't do nothing to those redskins at first. I mean there wasn't no plan or anything. . . ."

"What?"

"I told Johnny not to do nothing. The old man wasn't doing no harm. Just curious, he was, I told him. But he didn't pay no attention. Shot the old man."

"What old man? Davey, what in the hell are you talking about?"

"The redskin. Old man, gray hair he had. Must have been fifty years old, maybe more. He was trying to tell us something, but we couldn't make out what it was. Truth is, we didn't really care, neither one of us. I just wanted to push on, but Johnny was . . ."

"Johnny was what, Davey? What was Johnny doing? Come on, tell me what happened."

The man shook his head. "Well, I uhh . . . Johnny . . . he just started to bang away at the old man. Hit him three or four times. Killed him for sure."

"I didn't find anybody but you and Carlson," Slocum said. He knew time was wasting, but he wanted to learn as much as he could while the man was lucid. It appeared that Davey was just rambling, letting the truth trickle out of him the same way water had dribbled from the canteen. But as long as it was coming, Slocum was going to let it.

Keeping one eye on the valley behind and below him, he clapped the man on the shoulder. "What happened then?"

"We rode away. Johnny just giddyupped, and we rode away like nothing happened."

"You mean the other warriors let you do that?"

"There weren't any other redskins. The old man was alone. Nobody at all with him."

"So you left him there. . . ."

"What else could we do? He was gut shot. Johnny wanted to take his scalp, but I said it wasn't right. He just. . . ."

"Just what . . . ?"

"The old man didn't do nothing. Not a thing. Just jabberin' like he was tryin' to tell us something. . . ."

"When were you attacked?"

"About an hour later, I guess—I don't know." The man shifted his weight, and the movement speared through his wounded side, bringing a groan to his lips. "Longest god-damned hour I ever spent. I knew them redskins was gonna come, just knew it. I told Johnny we shouldn't go on no farther without an escort, but he just laughed."

He groaned again, then his head lolled to one side. He was out, and Slocum didn't bother to try to bring him to. There would be plenty of time for that once they were safe.

After checking the lashings once more, he climbed back onto the roan and moved out. The hair was still prickling on the back of his neck, but he had seen no one, not a thing to tell him why.

Entering the next valley, he spotted a stand of cotton-woods and a shallow creek, its sluggish current was winding through tall clumps of rushes. The brown cattails, their crowns of golden fluff all but gone, nodded in the breeze as Slocum headed toward the creek. It would be a chance to water the horses and refill the canteens for the rest of the trip, which threatened to be even longer than he had anticipated.

Keeping a weather eye out for any telltale sign, he urged the mounts toward the rushes, then pushed on through to the bank of the creek. The horses were thirsty, and he tugged the pack horse up close to the bank, and watched as it bent to drink. The roan, too, was nuzzling the clear but sluggish current.

Dropping to his knees, he opened both canteens and dunked them under the surface. He could hear the bubbling as air rushed out and the water burbled in. When they stopped bubbling, he pulled the canteens out one at a time, screwed the caps on, and slung them over his shoulder.

He was about to stand up when he heard a horse nicker. It came from somewhere behind him, and at first he wanted to shout, but then remembered his situation. Lowering the canteens to the ground, he crept to the roan, removed his Winchester from the scabbard and levered a shell into the chamber.

The horse nickered again, and he heard voices. At least two men were somewhere behind him in the grass. Easing through the cattails to a point where he could see through the last thin veil of stalks, he spotted two Sioux warriors on their ponies. The ponies weren't painted for war, and the warriors' faces were free of paint as well.

The Sioux didn't sound as if they were worried about giving themselves away. For a moment, he thought maybe they didn't know he was there, but then realized it might be a trick. If they could decoy him into giving his location away, others might be out there in the grass somewhere, waiting to overwhelm him. It made sense that these men had been following him. It explained the almost palpable and incontrovertible tingling he'd felt off and on for the last few miles, as if he had known they were there without having to see them.

The Sioux were moving toward the creek, laughing quietly. If it was an act, it was a damn good one, Slocum thought. He glanced back at the horses, and saw that the Sioux would come to the edge of the creek not more than fifty yards away from them. He wanted to turn and run to the animals, but there was no way he could get to them without calling attention to himself.

He saw the limp form of the unconscious teamster, and knew that he couldn't leave Chilton like that—defenseless and unarmed. The warriors pushed through the reeds, the stiff blades rattling and slapping as the ponies shouldered their way through them. Slocum gripped his Winchester tightly, and took advantage of the racket of the ponies' passage to ease back toward the water's edge.

Conscious of his teeth grinding together, Slocum loosened his jaw, heard it crack under his right ear, and held his breath, thinking that the noise would have been loud enough for the Sioux to hear. But the warriors dismounted, letting their ponies drink. Both of them disappeared from his view, and Slocum guessed they had knelt beside the creek to get drinks for themselves.

Then the roan, aware of the interlopers, nickered, and Slocum heard one of the warriors hush the other. A couple of syllables drifted toward him, but he didn't know the Lakota language, and all he could do was wait.

Then, he heard the sound of water splashing. Peering through the curtain of quivering reeds, he waited for the first glimpse of color or movement. It seemed to take forever, then a shadow darkened the pale green veil for a moment, and he caught the outline of a man. He was crouched at the waist, one arm extended before him as he moved past, walking parallel to the creek.

Slocum knew the warriors must have seen the horses by now, and he started to bring up the Winchester. He drew a bead on the shadow moving past, saw it stop for a moment, then turn back. He heard footsteps in the creek, and suddenly the two Sioux popped into view over the tops of the reeds. They must have mounted their ponies, Slocum thought.

He waited for a shout that would bring others running, but all he heard was a sudden hiss as the ponies charged back through the reeds and out into the tall grass away from the creek.

"What the hell is going on?" Slocum whispered.

He watched the two Sioux charge through the grass and start up the slope. They had made no movement toward

Slocum's horses, other than locating them, then they bolted. Slocum couldn't figure it out. Backing through the reeds, he nearly lost his footing on the soft sand at the edge of the creek. He caught himself by snatching at a handful of the reeds, and took a deep breath.

The two Sioux were rapidly disappearing toward the ridge line and a moment later, they were outlined starkly against the dark blue of the sky, then they disappeared over the far side.

There was no time to waste. Slocum sprang into the saddle, snatched at the rope lead for the pack horse, and kicked the roan into a full gallop. He had to get out of the valley before the Sioux returned.

4

The rest of the ride back to camp was an anticlimax. Slocum found himself looking over his shoulder every few yards expecting to see the Sioux in hot pursuit. But every time he turned around, he was simply staring into the emptiness of the sea of grass. If the Sioux were following him, they were staying well out of sight.

It was nearly sundown by the time he rode up the last rise before the survey team's work camp. From the ridge, he could see the huge fire below, and several men arranged around it as if they were afraid of the dark. They leaned in toward the flames, and their heads bobbed in earnest conversation. Slocum knew they were as afraid of the silence as they were of the dark.

Somewhere beyond the circle cast by the fire, he knew four sentries were posted, and he knew those men were even more frightened than those huddled around the fire. They were the first line of defense and, as such, would be the first to die in the event of an enemy attack. There was even the possibility that they might not realize it until the knife had severed their throats, or pierced a vital organ.

The flash of pain would be the first warning, and the last sensation.

That fear gave the men hair-trigger reactions. It was something they all shared; something they all suffered from. Whoever drew sentry duty seemed to put on nerves like a suit of clothes, and they'd wear it until relieved. They were given to discharging their weapons into the night, killing shadows, shooting at the whisper of passing wings, or the sound of the wind in the grass. As he started down toward the camp, he knew that he would have to warn the sentries of his approach.

The sun slipped away suddenly, its last rays spearing up at the heavens from behind purple clouds in one last desperate attempt to hold off the night. Then the darkness seemed to wrap him like a blanket, and he drew his Colt Navy as he eased down to the flats of the valley bottom. He fired into the air and shouted, then he fired again.

He heard shouts and saw the men scatter from around the flames, seeking the safety of the darkness until their sudden terror could be addressed.

Drawing closer, he called out, "Hello! Slocum here. I need help!" He fired one more shot. He could hear footsteps then, their pounding muffled by the thick carpet of grass. A pair of shadows flitted across the fire, and for a moment, they were outlined with orange coronas before they disappeared again.

"Slocum, what's wrong?" someone called. He thought he recognized the voice. It's lilt, decidedly Irish, sounded like that of Barney Tormey.

"That you, Barney?"

"Aye, lad. What's wrong?"

"Got a wounded man here. He's hurt pretty bad. Get the doc, would you?"

Now that the camp knew he posed no threat, he whipped the roan into a gallop, and glanced back at the follow horse, who was little more than a clot of shadow bounding along behind him like a hellhound.

He headed toward the camp fire. Men were materializing out of the shadows again, gathering around the fire and staring into the darkness toward him. Behind them, he saw the figure of Amos Coburn, the surgeon, come shuffling out of the darkness. When he reached the open ground around the fire, he slowed the roan, then slid from the saddle. The men rushed in around him like a flood tide, one taking the reins, another handing him a cup of coffee, a third slapping him on the back.

Barney stepped up to him, glanced past him, and asked, "Who's that, lad?"

Slocum shook his head. "Davey Chilton. He was one of the teamsters on the supply wagon. There was some trouble, which I don't quite understand, and he's been hurt pretty badly."

"Hurt how?"

"Shot. With an arrow."

Tormey nodded. "What about the other man? Johnny Carlson? Where's he?"

"Dead. We'll have to go back and bury him tomorrow. I didn't want to take the time. I had to get this man to some medical help, and there was a chance that the Indians were still around."

"Redskins, was it, then?"

"Yeah. Sioux, I think. It was a Sioux arrow I pulled out of him, and there were several more in the wagon. They were charred, but I could still see the markings under the feathers. They sure as hell looked like Sioux."

"This is Sioux country, after all," Tormey said. "Could be Crow, maybe, but most likely Sioux or Cheyenne."

"The Crows are friendly, I thought," Slocum said. "Anyway, the two braves who followed me were Sioux. I don't know whether they were the same ones who attacked the wagon, but I guess there's a good chance they were."

"So you got yourself a good look at the noble red men, did you?"

"Not for the first time, Barney. You ought to know that. You can't spend any time on the Plains without running into an Indian or two now and then."

"Aye, that's so. But I'll wager it's the first time you saw their handiwork close up."

"Wrong again. We better get this man off the horse. He's been bleeding off and on all day. I don't know whether he'll make it or not. I tried to take it easy on him, but it was a long, hard ride."

He turned then, but the wounded man was already off the horse and lying on a blanket on the ground. Amos Coburn was kneeling beside him slitting the man's bloody shirt open. A black bag yawned open beside the gangly physician, and his spectacles glinted in the firelight as he twisted his head back and forth on his slender neck. He looked up at Slocum and said, "You did a pretty fair job of keeping the bleeding under control, Johnny. Probably saved his life."

"He'll make it then?"

"Now, I didn't say that, did I? But if he does, it's you he'll have to thank."

"It looked like a pretty clean wound, Doc. The arrow went clear through. I just snapped off the arrowhead, pulled it out, and put pressure bandages on both holes. Not much more than blind luck if it did any good for him."

"Blind luck or no, he's got a chance, and that's more than he would have had if you left the damn arrow in him." He swabbed the wounds, now bared to the firelight, with wadded gauze and whiskey.

Chilton rolled his head from side to side, and every time Coburn poured a little more whiskey on one of the wounds, he moaned.

"See there, Johnny, he's still alive, boy," Tormey said. "Looks to me like you done all right by him. You should be proud of yourself."

"What I should be is asleep," Slocum said, taking a sip of hot coffee. He let the scalding liquid slide down his throat, and inhaled sharply to cool its passage as best as he could, but then took another sip immediately.

"Past your bedtime, is it now? Well, well, well, I thought you were a grown man, man of the world, even. Or at least of this godforsaken patch of it, anyway."

"What I am is one tired cowboy, Barney. I got to get some sleep before I collapse."

"We'll be talking in the morning, I expect. Mr. Anderson'll be here around ten. I imagine he'll be wanting to send for the cavalry, and he won't want to do that unless he knows what's what. I'll let you sleep until he gets here, even if I have to sit in front of your tent with a shotgun on me lap."

Slocum patted the portly Irishman on the shoulder. "A lap like that should be able to hold a howitzer, Barney. Or at least a Gatling gun."

"Do you think so? Maybe I should talk to Phil Sheridan, see if he can use me."

"I don't think he could afford to feed you, Barney."

Tormey laughed, and Slocum walked off to his tent. He didn't really want to sleep because he wasn't looking forward to the morning, but his body was about to stop moving on its own, and he figured he might as well lie down.

Tossing and turning for an hour or so, he ran over the day's events in his head. He was troubled by the story the teamster had told him, or more accurately, the story that had to be shaken out of the wounded man like change from the pocket of a pair of pants.

It was dangerous enough being where they were. There was a treaty that prohibited white men from using the Powder River country for anything at all without Sioux permission. In fact, they weren't even allowed to *be* there without permission. But the know-it-alls in Washington wanted the Northern Pacific built, and they wanted it in a hurry. If the Indians won't give permission, then build it anyway. Worrying about trouble when it came seemed to be the prevailing wisdom.

If what the teamster had told him was even halfway accurate, then trouble was on its way. Trespassing on Sioux lands was bad enough, but shooting an old man to death without provocation was stirring the coals under an already boiling pot.

He drifted off without having any better understanding of what had happened, and feeling no better about what lay ahead.

He was awakened early. There was some sort of ruckus in the camp; he heard angry voices snarling at one another and sharp exchanges in evident anger. He couldn't catch the words, but the tone told him all he needed to know.

He dressed quickly, and walked out of his tent into a brilliant sunlight that made him wince. Shielding his eyes, he spotted a knot of men, obviously the source of the noise, and ambled toward it.

One of the arguers spotted him, and pushed through the tight ring surrounding the center of the storm. "Here comes Slocum. Ask him!"

Another of the arguers, Warren Anderson, followed the first man into the clear. Anderson was the head of the survey crew. He was more than a foreman, but not quite a member of the brass. He was fairly short-tempered, a fact which did not endear him to the men, but Slocum had found him to be fair-minded and easy to get along with.

"John," Anderson said, "how you feeling this morning?"

"Just about like I been trampled by a herd of cattle," Slocum answered.

Anderson turned to one of the men straggling in his wake. "Get him some coffee, would you, Pete?"

Pete Jolly scurried away like a dim-witted squirrel, his head bobbing as he repeated the order to himself three or four times. He was back a moment later, a tin mug of coffee in his hand. In the bright sunlight, the steam curling off the surface was almost transparent. He thrust the mug at Slocum. "Real hot, it is," he said.

"Thanks, Pete," Slocum said, accepting the mug and making sure to hold it by its handle. After taking a sip, he said, "What can I do for you, Warren?"

"They tell me you're the one brought in Davey Chilton, that right?"

Slocum nodded. "Guess so."

"I hear you saw who done it, too—is that right?"

"No, it isn't. Whatever happened had already happened by the time I got to the wagon. I saw what had been done, but it was all over before I got there."

"I thought you saw a couple of Sioux bucks?"

Slocum sipped more of his coffee. "I did, but I have no reason to think they were the ones that attacked the wagon and killed Carlson. They could have been, but I just don't know that for sure."

"The wagon was burned, one man killed—cooked alive from what I hear—and another gut shot with a Sioux arrow. Seems pretty clear to me what happened. The Sioux you saw must have been the ones who did it. Don't seem to me there's any other explanation."

"This is Sioux country, Warren. There's thousands of Indians out there on the Plains, and why not? It's their land. As near as I could tell, Carlson was dead before the wagon burned. He had a couple of arrows sticking in him. Most likely, they torched the wagon just before leaving. But you should talk to Chilton, see what he can tell you, before you go off looking for trouble."

Anderson snorted. "Already talked to Chilton. That's why I'm sending to Fort McAllister for the army."

"I don't think we need to do that, Mr. Anderson. It's asking for trouble."

"Trouble's already come, John. What we got to do now is shut it down before it gets out of hand."

"You say you already talked to Chilton. He tell you about the old man?"

"What old man?"

"He told me an old Indian came up to the wagon. He was trying to tell them something, but didn't have any English. Carlson shot him for no reason."

Anderson shook his head. "That's not what happened, John. Chilton was clear about that. He said a bunch of Sioux jumped the wagon without any warning."

"That's not what he told me."

"He was delirious when he talked to you, most likely, and since he was there and you weren't, I got to take his word for it."

"What about the old man?"

"You find a dead Indian out there?"

Slocum shook his head. "Nope."

"Well there you are, then. We'll let the cavalry handle it. Meantime, I'd like you to take a burial detail out there and see to it Carlson gets put under proper."

"But I—"

"Just do it, John, would you please?"

5

Slocum picked two men for the burial detail. Clay Randall and Newt Parsons were young and eager. Randall had the shoulders of a plowboy and fair hair so fine it looked like a baby's. His big blue eyes always seemed wide open in surprise or astonishment. Newt Parsons had the sunburned skin of a kid who was new to the sun. He was half Randall's size, and had restless gray eyes.

They chattered about the possibility of running into hostile Indians, and each time Slocum tried to convince them it was unlikely, they nodded in agreement. But a moment later, they would be back to their mindless prattle. Slocum was tempted to leave them behind and go do the job himself, but he knew Warren Anderson would never permit it, and Slocum needed his job. Tough-minded as he was, Anderson didn't like to be crossed, and when he gave an order, he expected that it would be carried out, with all the *i*'s dotted and all the *t*'s crossed.

They were already on their horses when Anderson reappeared. "John, I want you to take more than two men with you."

"No need, Warren."

"Maybe not, but I want you to do it anyhow." Without waiting for an argument, he bellowed, "Peters, Higgins, get your asses over here."

The two men sprinted up, expectant looks on their faces. Slocum didn't care for either one. Win Peters and Jack Higgins were two of the more boisterous men in the camp. Peters was a boss on the survey team, and as much as he knew about topography, he knew even more about the inside of a bottle. Slocum tried to recall a day on which Peters hadn't had at least one drink, and decided that if there had been such a day, it must have been before the war.

Jack Higgins was a mean-tempered bully. Short and potbellied, he liked to throw his weight around, particularly among the younger men. Most of them were only too happy to do what he said because it was well known that Higgins had killed two men with his bare hands. Slocum was more than willing to bet it wasn't a fair fight on either occasion.

Planting himself in front of Slocum's horse, Anderson said, "You boys are gonna go with John, here. Do what he says. He's in charge. Anything he tells you, it's the same as if I told you myself. Got that straight?"

Higgins glared at Slocum before nodding. "Got it, Mr. Anderson," he said.

Win Peters took off his hat and ran a fistful of fingers through his red hair. "Where we goin', Mr. Anderson?"

"Gonna bury Johnny Carlson. Bring extra rounds for your rifle, in case there's trouble."

"I'm sure there won't be any trouble, Warren," Slocum assured him.

"Probably not, but I want you to play it safe. You see any redskins, you run for it, understand?"

Slocum nodded.

"By the time you get back, the army'll be here. I sent a rider to Fort McAllister. They'll be sending a detachment of cavalry. Should be more than enough, but I won't rest easy until the troopers get here. Don't give me cause to worry about anything else, if you can help it, John."

Higgins and Peters sprinted off to get their horses, and Slocum waited impatiently. He didn't like the idea of bringing in the army any more than he liked the idea of having a pair of hot-tempered no-accounts on the burial detail. If the idea was to avoid trouble, Anderson was sending the wrong men along. He debated meeting Anderson halfway, exchanging Peters and Higgins for two other more dependable men but Anderson seemed like he was in no mood for discussion.

When the two men reappeared on their mounts, Slocum led the way out of camp at a trot. He wanted to put some distance between himself and Anderson before the boss could decide to complicate matters still further.

Once out on the Plains, Slocum settled into a steady pace, staying out in front of the four men. He wasn't talkative in the best of situations, and he had little to say to any of the men trailing behind him. If he could get Carlson into the ground and get back without having to say a word, that would suit him just fine.

Unencumbered, it was a five hour ride. Slocum allowed himself to bask in the sun, and soak up the vistas of rolling hills and seemingly endless grass. The four men of the burial detail stayed a few yards behind him, talking among themselves. He caught snatches, not much, but enough to know they were trying to outdo one another in what would happen should they run into a band of Sioux. Rather then try to talk them out of it, he figured it was better to let them talk it out. The last thing he wanted to happen was to run into a war party and have to keep control of their mindless bravado.

It was near two when they broke over the ridge above the valley where the wagon lay. The wreckage was hidden by trees, and Slocum raised a hand to halt his team. He knew the Sioux might be watching; perhaps they were expecting some white men to return for the dead man, either to take him away, or to bury him.

Using the field glasses, he swept the valley floor from end to end, paying particular attention to the brush thickets and stands of willows and cottonwoods. They were the only cover the valley offered, and in the thickest undergrowth, a sizable party of men could easily stay hidden. The willows waved in the wind, but the only signs of life were the darting flights of birds flitting from tree to tree, or disappearing behind the brush to land on the creek bank for a drink.

He couldn't be sure, but it looked as if the valley was deserted. Dropping the field glasses back into his saddle-bags, he turned to look at the four men arrayed behind him in a straight line.

"See anything?" Win Peters asked.

Slocum shook his head. "Nope. Not a blessed thing. Looks like we're alone."

"Don't matter whether we are or not," Higgins said. "Ain't likely the Sioux would bother five men with repeating rifles. In fact, I kinda wish they would. Teach them savages a lesson they won't forget too quick."

"We're here to bury Johnny Carlson, not to start a war. Remember that!" Slocum snapped. "Now, let's get on down there and get it done."

"Scared of the redskins, are you, Slocum?" Higgins said. The others laughed, but it was a hollow, nervous giggle that died quickly.

"Any man in his right mind would be a little scared of them. Especially out here," Slocum answered.

Higgins shrugged. "Not me."

"Ever see a full-blown Sioux war party, Higgins?"

"Sure. The survey party gets hit all the time. You know that. Just a nuisance, is all."

"I mean a *real* war party. The kind Crazy Horse or Sitting Bull might lead, with a thousand warriors swarming like hornets, and arrows flying everywhere you look. The kind where you can't hear yourself think for the thunder of hooves, and the war cries drilling holes in your skull and freezing your heart right there in your chest. The kind where you go to sleep for weeks afterward hearing the sound of a half-dozen arrows punching their way through a man's rib cage, and then all you can hear is the bubbling in his lungs when he tries to breathe. You ever see a war party like that?"

Higgins looked nervous. He glanced at the men on either side of him. He knew they were waiting for his answer, and he also knew, his reputation was hanging by a slender thread. Taking a deep breath, he held it a moment, then nodded as he said, "Yeah, sure I've seen that. It didn't scare me none, neither."

"Well," Slocum drawled, "let's just hope you don't get to see it again. Let's go, then. Spread out and keep your eyes open. Watch the brush along the creek, and watch the ridge line. If they're waiting over there," he said, pointing to the opposite ridge, "we want as much warning as we can get."

At the bottom of the slope, the valley flattened out, and much of the opposite slope was hidden by the irregular line of trees. When he reached the brush, Slocum said, "I'll go first. You follow, one at a time." At least, by riding single file, they would make five separate targets instead of one.

He led the way through the brush, crossed the creek, and broke into the open grassland on the far side. The wagon was about seventy yards downstream, and Slocum glanced at it quickly before calling out, "Higgins, you're next!"

He heard the brush scrape against Higgins's legs, heard the splash as the horse waded across the creek, then more brush scraping. Higgins popped into view, his face tight. "Bring the others across one at a time," Slocum said. "I'll meet you at the wagon."

Without waiting for an answer, he wheeled the roan and nudged it into a walk. Something moved in the wagon bed, and he knew right away what it was. Drawing his Colt, he fired at the wagon bed. With a squawk and flutter of wings, two buzzards flopped out of the wagon. They glared at him a moment, and he drew a bead, fired again, and drilled the larger of the two birds.

The other bird screeched angrily and beat its wings. Then it half ran and half flew twenty yards away, barely clearing the tips of the blades of grass.

Dismounting, Slocum approached the wagon prepared for the worst. What he found surpassed his imagination. Carlson's carcass had been ripped open, and the charred flesh peeled back from his stomach. The dead man's entrails had been savaged by the birds, and strands of intestine glistened in the sunlight where they were draped over his hips and rib cage. And the buzzards hadn't even been there long.

Hearing the horses approach, he turned in time to see Higgins dismounting, with the other three men riding in a tight knot behind him.

"Buzzards got him, did they?" Higgins said. There was a hint of amusement in his voice, and Slocum glared at him.

"Get a shovel, Higgins."

Instead, Higgins walked over to the wagon and looked at Johnny Carlson, who was sprawled half in and half out of tilted bed. "Ain't a pretty sight, is he?" he said.

"Get a shovel, damn you!"

Higgins mumbled something, walked back to his horse and snatched at the shovel hanging from his saddle horn. He stood in front of Slocum, brandishing the shovel as if it were a club. "What next, boss?"

Peters had the second shovel and he approached the wagon trying not to look at Carlson's body. He whacked at the tall grass, then used the edge of the shovel to outline a three-by-six-foot rectangle. Without waiting for Slocum's direction, he started to peel back the turf.

Higgins, realizing that Slocum had said all he that was going to say, walked over to join Peters.

Slocum called to the other two men, who were still sitting on their horses, and they dismounted. "Take a walk up the slope a way," he said. "Just far enough that you can see over the trees to the other side of the creek. Keep a sharp lookout. You see anything that doesn't look right, give a holler."

"Where you going, Mr. Slocum?" Newt Parsons asked.

Slocum gestured with his chin. "Going to ride up top of this ridge and take a look at the next valley."

"Don't want to get his hands dirty," Higgins said. "Too good to bend his back a little."

Slocum had had enough. He walked over to Higgins, planted himself squarely in front of him, and stepped into the still-shallow rectangle. "Look, Higgins, I've had about enough of you. I didn't want you on this trip anyway, but as long as you're here, do what you're told and keep your mouth shut."

"You're standing in a grave, Slocum," Higgins said, leaning on his shovel. "Don't tempt me."

"Just shut up, Jack," Parsons said. "It gets a little tiresome hearing you gripe all the time. Slocum's in charge. You heard Mr. Anderson say that. I heard it, we all did. Let's just do what we come to do and get the hell out of here. This place makes my skin crawl."

"You sound as lily-livered as Slocum here, Win. What's the matter, what he got catching?"

Slocum swung from the heels. He felt his fist crack sharply into Higgins's jaw. The sound was loud as a pistol shot. Higgins staggered a step and sat down hard. Reaching down with one hand to find his balance, he put his weight onto it and started to rise. He was already moving when he realized he had placed his palm over the outstretched hand of Johnny Carlson. "Jesus!" he shouted, jerking his hand away, and with it, his sole support. He sat down a second time.

Peters laughed.

"Johnny pinch you, did he, Jack?" He laughed, and Higgins glowered at him.

"You think it's funny, do you?"

"You got that right."

Slocum turned his back and started toward his horse.

"I'll remember that, Slocum," Higgins shouted after him. "Believe it!"

6

Slocum approached the ridge at an oblique angle. It was easier for the horse to make the climb that way. Just in case there were Sioux on the far side, he didn't want to have to make an abrupt turn. It would be far easier to sweep in a broad loop across the hillside and head back down to the creek.

A hundred yards from the top, he jerked the Winchester carbine from its boot, levered a round home, and braced it across his lap. He kept his right hand curled through the trigger guard, with a finger resting lightly on the trigger itself. Fifty yards from the top, he reined in and paused to listen.

The sound of the shovels hacking at the earth drifted toward him, carried by the breeze. He turned in the saddle to look at the burial team for a moment. Even at this distance, he could clearly see the outline of the grave. It appeared to be almost two feet deep now, and the mound of loose earth beside it was dark brown with dampness. For a moment, he imagined he could smell the richness of the earth, and it reminded him of long ago. He had loved to fish with his grandfather, and recalled the thrill of getting up just before daybreak, taking a lantern and a shovel, and digging in his mother's garden for worms.

He could still see the slick skin of a fat earthworm, with its pale skin orange in the lantern light, and the clot of red near its head almost the color of blood. For a moment, he could even feel the cool smoothness of a fat worm in his palm, the tickle as it wiggled and tried to squirm free.

Smiling, he remembered the first time he'd done the digging. Just barely managing to catch one of the fat worms, he'd tugged it from the ground, held it out, and asked his grandfather, "How does it know which end its head is, Grandpa?"

His grandfather had laughed until he almost choked. Then, he took the worm in his own callused hands which were cupped like a wooden bowl, and said, "He waits to see which way he's goin', Johnny. Then he knows for sure."

Slocum didn't permit himself the luxury of recollection very often. Whenever he succumbed to the temptation, all he succeeded in doing was making himself all too painfully aware of how long ago and far away his past now was. He would feel the pain for hours as he scrambled to shove the memories. Each time he hoped they'd smother and die, that they would never crawl like those slick, fat worms, into daylight again. But every time, he knew they would and that it would hurt just as much.

Trying now to push the thoughts of his grandfather aside, he clucked to the roan and eased it the rest of the way toward the ridge line. When he reached the crest, he reined in once more, dismounted, and walked across the flat top of the ridge pulling the roan along behind him. Being on foot made him nervous, but a man on horseback was too good a silhouette for a marksman below, and he'd have to risk it.

The top of the ridge was nearly two hundred yards across. It was almost flat, but not quite. He could feel the slight upward tilt in his feet as he walked. When the angle changed and started downhill, he let go of the reins, and left the roan to walk the rest of the way across alone.

Fifty yards from the far side, he lay down to crawl the last bit. Peering out into the valley, he realized it was almost a replica of the one behind him. A sluggish creek squirmed its way across the valley floor. Willows and cottonwoods waved in the breeze. The grass, lush, thick, and waist deep, swirled and dipped as the wind whispered across it.

But there was one difference.

On the bottom land, not far from the creek, a rough wooden structure stood on stilts about six feet high. It looked almost like a small shed with a flat roof but without walls. He knew right away what it was—a Sioux burial scaffold.

Slocum took a deep breath. Using the field glasses, he examined the platform. The oblong mound on top was the deceased, wrapped in a buffalo robe to keep away the carrion birds. He could see a lance, and what looked like one end of a bow, lying beside the body.

Several feathers fluttered in the breeze; they were dangling from the platform legs by string or buckskin thongs. Two small birds hopped across the buffalo skin, pecking at something. Probably bugs, Slocum thought.

Scanning the valley from end to end, Slocum looked for evidence of a human presence. He found none. Getting slowly to his feet, he continued to watch the platform. He was looking for something, but he didn't know what. There was just the nagging feeling that the platform meant something. Whistling for the roan, he looped the field glasses around his neck as he waited for the horse to amble over to him. He swung into the saddle, and booting the

Winchester, he urged the roan forward and started down into the valley.

For a moment, he thought about waiting to bring the others with him when they were done with the burial, but the thought of listening to Higgins expound on how many more Sioux he would like to see on similar platforms was enough to make him take the risk. He kept his eyes fixed on the platform as he eased down through the grass.

As he drew closer, he felt a profound sadness come over him. There was something terrible about being left out under the open sky. It didn't matter that there was a bow and lance, or that the dead man was securely wrapped in a buffalo hide. The sky above was so immense and empty, and the six feet from the ground to the platform seemed such an enormous distance, as if the dead warrior was floating in a void, too far from the ground or sky, adrift and alone.

When he reached the small ground swell on which the platform had been built, he dismounted and walked the last few yards. He didn't know much about Sioux customs, and even less about their burial practices. But he knew that graves were sacred sites for them, as they were for all people, and the thought filled him with awe.

Bringing his rifle, he swung up onto the platform. He felt it was almost sacrilegious, but he had to know who lay there so desolately. Thongs held the robe closed, and he struggled with the knots for a moment. He heard the wind then for a moment, a fierce gust that seemed to sweep into the valley out of nowhere, as if warning him to stop the profanation. But he pushed on.

One thong came loose, and he started on a second knot. He had to see for himself, had to know—he just had to. Loosening the thongs, he grasped a flap of the buffalo hide, felt the long, soft hairs and, beneath them, the shorter, thicker ones that made the hide so valuable in winter. Opening the buffalo robe, he found himself staring into the wizened features of an old man, and he knew then that the story Dave Chilton had told him had not been delirium. This was the man that Johnny Carlson had killed. It had to be. There was no way that he could prove it, but it had to be. The stench of death swirled around him, and he had to struggle to keep from gagging.

Closing the robe again, he made sure the leather thongs were knotted securely, his fingers seemed stiff and awkward in his haste. He dropped to the ground, then reached up for his Winchester feeling as if he'd just done something terrible. Sin was not a notion he paid much attention to. Life was too hard and too dangerous for such niceties, but that's what he felt like he had done all the same— committed a sin.

Bowing his head, he mumbled an apology to God or Wakan Tanka, or whatever spirit it was that kept watch on this desolate resting place. He walked back to the roan which seemed to be watching him, its look almost judgmental. He knew he was imagining things by making the horse accuse him the way he accused himself. "What the hell are you looking at?" he mumbled.

He booted the Winchester, looped the reins, and put a foot in the stirrup, when he saw something moving in the brush down by the creek. He stopped, redrew the carbine, and stared at the place where he'd seen the movement. There was no sign of anyone, and the valley was perfectly still. A bird trilled for a moment, then darted out of a cottonwood and swooped along the top of the brush to land in a willow fifty yards away.

When Slocum finished tracking the flight of the bird, he looked back to the brush. A flash of color behind shimmering leaves caught his attention. He gripped the

Winchester tightly, dropped to one knee behind the roan, and trained his sights on the dash of red.

Thumbing back the hammer, he held his breath, waiting for what—a charge, a rifle shot, maybe a hail of arrows? Letting his breath out slowly, he squinted into the undergrowth, starting to doubt he had seen anything all. A war party would have made its move by now, he thought.

Standing up, he started toward the color. With every step, he expected to see someone, to hear something, anything, to tell him that he was not imagining things. Closer and closer, the Winchester held loosely now, not even aimed at his destination.

Then with a rush, the brush lashed back and forth and he heard someone splash into the creek beyond the trees. Slocum rushed forward, using the rifle to sweep the branches aside. He plunged into the water. Twenty yards away, legs working like pistons, a woman struggled to run through the creek. Water splashed in every direction, with sheets catching the light and rippling like silver foil.

"Stop!" he shouted. "Wait!"

He was being reckless, and when the thought finally registered, he realized that he didn't care. He plunged after the fleeing women, lifting his legs high in the air to leap through the water. He was closing the gap, his long strides bringing him closer and closer every second.

She turned then, and her eyes were wide with terror.

"Stop!" he shouted once more, realizing that she wouldn't, and probably even couldn't, fear and terror were driving her.

Heading for the bank, she slipped and fell, and he was on her in three strides as she tried to claw her way out of the creek and up onto the sandy bank.

It dawned on him suddenly that she hadn't screamed. That almost certainly meant that she was alone. There was no point in screaming if there was no one to hear. No one knew that better than a Sioux woman. As he bent to grab her shoulder, she turned on him, her teeth bared. Then, the bright blade of a knife suddenly sliced the air in front of him, turning him to stone.

She crawled up the slope backward. Her buckskin dress was darkened by the water, and looked impossibly heavy. Water streamed from it, leaving behind tiny drops glittering like diamonds among the beadwork. Her coal-black hair hung over her shoulders, and was braided into twin columns that looked like obsidian laced with beaded bands.

Slocum held a hand up, palm toward her, fingers splayed. "Wait," he said, "I won't hurt you."

He smiled, and she sliced the air between them with the knife again. He backed away a step. She got to her knees, and he could hear her panting. She licked her lips, then wiped a stray strand of hair out of her eyes with a sleeve. Her eyes never left his face.

"Do you speak English?" he asked.

She glared at him.

"English?" he asked again.

She nodded her head. "Yes."

"I won't hurt you. I'm sorry if I frightened you."

She continued to pant, but her breathing was slowly returning to normal. Her teeth were clenched, and her knuckles white around the handle of the knife. She seemed to be looking past him, as if searching for something, or as if she couldn't stand to look at him directly.

"The warrior on the scaffold, was he your father?"

"Scaffold?" She questioned the strange word.

He pointed back toward where the platform was, although it could not be seen. "The burial platform. The man in the buffalo robe, was he your father?"

She shook her head.

"Grandfather?" he guessed.

She nodded. "Grandfather. . . ." The word seemed to catch in her throat. A moment later, tears were streaming down her cheeks. "I watched you," she said. "You shouldn't have. . . ."

"I know. I'm sorry, but I . . ."

"It's bad medicine," she said. "It's not right to do what you did."

"I know, and I'm sorry. But I had to see for myself who it was."

"Why? You did not know him. I have never seen you before, not even at the white man fort. Never." The last word was like a curse in its vehemence.

"How did he die?" Slocum asked.

"White men shot him."

"The men in the wagon?"

She nodded. "He did nothing to them. He went to them for help, but they shot him. For no reason."

"Help?"

She nodded again. "Yes. And he got the white man's help for the Sioux. . . ."

"And the white men got the Sioux thank you for their trouble."

"Yes." She smiled bitterly. "Yes, they got the thank you. The one that they should have got."

"Do you know who killed the white men?"

She tilted her head back. At first he thought she was going to laugh, or maybe even answer his question. But she did neither. She sprang to her feet and started to run, her passage through the brush sounding like sudden thunder.

He made no move to stop her.

7

Slocum stood there, knee-deep in the creek, until he could no longer hear the woman's passage through the brush. Only when she had vanished so completely that she may never have been there did it strike him how beautiful she was. He found himself wondering where she was going, if there was someone to take care of her, and would she be all right? Then he realized what a fool he was. She could not have been alone. At the moment, she might very well be on her way back to a nearby war party or village and immediately after she arrived a swarm of warriors would spring to the backs of their ponies, and come howling after him.

He remembered the burial detail in the next valley, and the realization that he, Higgins, Peters, and the others might end up like Johnny Carlson seemed to galvanize him. He stumbled out of the creek, and ran tearing through the brush as if he meant to uproot it all, then he broke into the clear. The first thing he saw was the scaffold, and it froze him for a split second. Then he saw the roan, and sprinted toward it, giving a piercing whistle to call the horse to him.

Leaping into the saddle, he roweled the roan's flanks,

then lashed it with the reins. Jerking hard, he turned the big stallion and charged up the slope. The horse took the climb in its stride and was barely winded when he reached the crest of the ridge.

In the valley below, he saw the four men sitting some distance away from the wreckage. The ruined wagon, its blackened shell like a scar against the lush green, drew his eye. Then, like a magnet, the dark brown mound of fresh earth captured his gaze.

He pushed the horse over the crest and down the far side of the ridge. The men saw him coming and jumped to their feet. He waved his arms to signal them to mount up. At first, they seemed uncertain as to what he wanted, and started to run toward him, but he waved them back frantically, and they turned back and mounted their horses.

The big roan was breathing hard under the incessant lashing of the reins, and Slocum bent low in the saddle to cut down on the wind resistance, making it easier for the horse. The burial team started toward him at a trot, but Slocum didn't bother to slow down. Every yard he put between himself and the scaffold of the old man was a yard farther out of harm's way.

When he finally reached the others, he reined in hard, and the roan reared up to get away from the bit.

"What's the matter?" Higgins sneered, "see your granny's shadow?"

Slocum ignored the gibe. "I found a Sioux burial scaffold in the next valley," he said.

Clay Randall's eyes lit up. "Heard about them, but I never seen one. Let's go take a look."

"No way," Slocum said. "We're getting the hell out of here."

"What's your hurry?" Higgins asked.

"I ran into a Sioux near the scaffold."

"We didn't hear nothing. How come you didn't shoot him?"

"Her," Slocum corrected.

"All right, her. How come you didn't shoot her? A redskin's a redskin, man or woman," Higgins said.

Slocum glared at the man and thought about giving him a lecture, but he realized he'd have more luck talking to the old man on the scaffold than he would have talking to Jack Higgins. Some men just didn't get it, and no matter how hard you tried, you couldn't get through to them. If there was a better example of a rock-hard skull than Jack Higgins's, Slocum wanted to meet him. He settled for saying, "I doubt the woman was alone."

"He's got a point," Parsons said. "Shoot her, and we might have a whole passel of angry bucks around our necks in nothing flat."

"We still might," Slocum said. "She ran off. I didn't see anyone else, but it's likely she wasn't alone. We better move it."

"You spook too easily, Slocum," Higgins insisted. "I swear, I never seen the like of it. A full-growed white man afraid of a squaw. Little slip of thing she was, most likely, and Slocum here is shakin' in his boots."

"Higgins," Slocum snapped, "I've had just about enough out of you. One more word, and I don't care what it is, or who you say it to, and I swear I will kill you. Do you understand me?"

Higgins said nothing.

"Do you?"

Higgins nodded. "I hear you. That don't mean I'm payin' no attention, but I hear you loud and clear. We'll see about this later."

Slocum nodded toward the end of the valley. "Let's get moving," he said.

He nudged the roan into motion without waiting for an answer. Looking toward the valley mouth, he reined in abruptly. "Company's coming," he said, pointing toward the northern end of the nearest ridge.

Outlined against the sky, there were several horsemen. They were clearly Indian, probably Sioux who had just been alerted by the woman he had seen. They were riding parallel to the hilltop, and were making no effort to close in on Slocum and his men. It seemed almost too pat, as if they were deliberately calling attention to themselves.

"We can outrun them," Peters said.

Slocum shook his head. "I think that's what they want us to do."

"Then let's show them we can take a hint," Higgins said.

"Slocum means he thinks it's a trap," Peters suggested. "And he's probably right. I know you hate to agree with him, but they probably got more braves just outside the valley. We run for it, we run smack into an ambush. We ought to sit here and pot them long range."

"I've got a better idea," Slocum said. "I think we ought to run right at them."

Higgins objected with a vigorous shake of his head. "They've got the high ground. We charge up that hill, our horses will be slower than they will on the flat. They can just sit there and wait for us to get close, then pick us off one by one."

"They won't," Slocum insisted. "That's not the way they fight. They want the advantage. They don't think of war the way we do. To them, honor and showing courage are more important than killing. In fact, they'd rather ride past you and tap you with a bow or a bare hand than shoot you."

"You can't lift a man's hair if you pat him on the back with your bare hand," Higgins argued.

"No, but a real Sioux would rather have a coup feather than a scalp any day."

Peters lifted his hat and ran a hand through the greasy red tangle of his hair. "Checkin' for feathers," he said. "I think we . . ."

"I don't reckon I got to go along with Slocum," Higgins said. "Hair, feathers, I don't give a damn. I just don't want to give them savages a chance to lift it. Just as soon keep what I got under my hat. I'm gonna make a run for it. Anybody wants to is welcome to join me. Most likely, there ain't nobody outside the valley. I think them bucks on the hill is the sum total of it."

"I'm going with Mr. Slocum," Randall said.

"Me too," Newt put in.

"I reckon I'll string along with you all," Peters chimed in. "Jack, you ought to come with us. I think Slocum's got the right idea."

"The hell with that. I wouldn't follow him around the corner for a drink, let alone into a passel of wild Injuns. I know what I'm doing. You go along with Slocum if you want, but not me."

"Time's awasting," Slocum said. "Let's move." He dug his spurs into the roan, sending it spurting toward the rise. Behind him, he heard an assortment of clucks and yips as the others got their own mounts in motion.

Glancing back, he saw Jack Higgins striking out on his own, lashing his horse and heading toward the valley mouth.

The Sioux on the hilltop slowed, then stopped altogether. Charging up the slope, Slocum watched them closely. So far, they showed no inclination to come downhill. It wasn't clear whether they were simply going to wait until the advancing quartet drew within reasonable range of guns and bows, or if they had something else in mind.

Slocum looked again to see where Higgins was, and spotted him galloping full tilt toward the mouth of the valley. Pulling his Winchester, Slocum turned to tell the others to do the same. The Sioux were still a half mile away, and they seemed as if they were determined to sit right where they were.

As the gap closed, one of the warriors turned his pony and raced along the ridge away from the mouth of the valley. Slocum aimed and fired, knowing that he was still two or three hundred yards out of effective range.

The gunshot echoed across the hillside, but provoked no return fire from the war party. There was no mistaking the fact that that's exactly what it was. The Sioux ponies were decorated on their flanks and chests with bright splotches of color. Lightning bolts, spots, and the imprints of hands, were all starkly painted in bright reds, whites, and yellows on the brown and white pintos.

The men behind Slocum loosed a volley, but like his own shot, it fell far short. This time, as if reluctant to ignore the challenge, several of the warriors returned fire. The crackle of gunfire, like the clapping of distant hands, seemed faint, even half-hearted.

Slocum was just six hundred yards from the war party now. Another one hundred yards, and he'd have to think seriously about changing direction. His thought had been to send the Indians scurrying on their way, and so far he'd failed miserably. They showed no sign of cracking.

Then a solitary Indian broke the opposite way, and galloped past the main body, which immediately broke into a fast trot behind him. Slocum angled across the hillside, heading for a point that would intercept them just above the opening into the broad valley. The Sioux refused to increase their pace, and now he was closing on them rapidly.

Suddenly, the entire war party angled away from him and

disappeared over the far side of the ridge. He slowed a little, thinking there might be a larger party lying in wait beyond the crest. Changing direction once more, he veered to the left and headed away from the place where the war party had vanished.

Reaching the crest, he reined in. The Sioux were several hundred yards away, their ponies running flat out. They too had veered left, and he watched as they thundered past the burial scaffold, and charged into the brush and on through the creek.

When the Sioux reappeared beyond the trees, he veered right. "Let's make a break for it," he yelled.

Following the crest, he kept one eye on the valley to the left, glancing behind him every fifty yards to make sure the others were staying with him.

Higgins was nowhere to be seen now, having passed out of the entrance to the valley. Nearing the end of the ridge he started downhill, avoiding the more precipitous descent where the sides of the valley mouth grew too step for secure footing.

It was then that he heard the war whoops. At first, he couldn't tell from which direction they were coming. He turned to look back, but the valley to the left was deserted. Gunfire crackled then, mixed with the yips and howls.

More gunshots, then silence.

"Higgins!" he shouted, lashing the roan and rocking in the saddle in a futile effort to get even more speed out of the big horse.

There was one more shot, then a single war cry which rose and and then grew faint, almost as if a great bird had given vent to it as it climbed out of earshot.

Far across the floor of the next valley, he saw half a dozen ponies running parallel to the creek. They were loping easily, as if their riders were in no hurry. Reaching the valley floor, he headed for the trees. Far ahead he saw a solitary horse, its head bobbing as it grazed on the rich grass. There was no doubt in his mind that it belonged to Jack Higgins.

Using reins and spurs together, he squeezed even more speed out of the roan. The saddle horse looked up as Slocum and his men approached, then, realizing the men were no threat, went back to grazing.

Slocum saw Higgins when he was still two hundred yards away. At one hundred yards, he knew the man was dead. At fifty yards, he slowed the roan to a walk. "Wait here," he said, as Peters pulled in alongside him.

At twenty-five yards, he stopped. He shielded his eyes from the glint of sunlight on white bone that was smeared with blood. Higgin's hat lay on its crown beside it. Slocum dismounted and walked the last ten yards. Turning to his men, he yelled, "Bring the shovels."

8

Slocum noticed the troopers while still a mile away from the camp. A red and white guidon had been planted in the center of half a dozen tents and it fluttered in the breeze. From that distance, the milling of the uniformed cavalrymen looked like the frenzied scurrying of large blue ants.

It was near sundown, and a large fire was already burning. Its light was feeble against the last hour of daylight. Even the soldiers seemed to be more comfortable near the blaze.

Win Peters had noticed them, too. "Now maybe we'll get some action," he said.

"Haven't you had enough action, Win?" Slocum asked.

"Damn it all, John, we just buried two men. Got a third that may not make it right there in camp. What does it take for you to understand we got us a small war on our hands, whether we like or not?"

"What troubles me," Slocum answered, "is that I think maybe you *do* like it—a lot. And I can promise you that no good will come of it."

"Look, you're just a hired gun, as far as I can see it. You don't give a damn whether we get this railroad built or not. If the tracks ended in the middle of nowhere—a pile of ties layin' there to rot, a stack of rails rustin' away to nothin'—that'd be just fine by you. But the rest of us, we got a stake in this thing. This is our lives, damn it."

"Your lives, maybe, but not your land, Win. You know that as well as I do."

"That's none of our affair. Our job is to survey the route so they can lay the damn track, and move on."

"What about the people who *can't* move on, the people who live here already? What are they supposed to do?"

"Hell, we got plows aplenty back east. Let 'em learn how to drag one. This is good land, good farming land. Nothing says they can't learn how, if they want to. But they're stubborn cusses. They don't want to learn. They want to stay like they always been, and they don't want to change—but they got to. That's not my fault."

"Let me ask you something, Win," Slocum said. "Suppose you were sitting back there in Ohio and a bunch of Sioux rode up to your daddy's farm. Suppose they burned the barn, burned the crops, killed your livestock, and handed you a bow and arrow and told you you had to hunt buffalo for a living. How do you suppose you'd like that?"

Peters shook his head. "That ain't the point, John, and you know it. You know exactly what I'm trying' to say, but you want to make it tough on me."

"It is *exactly* the point! You're trying to tell these people how to live. You wouldn't let anybody tell you, but you think it's all right for you to tell somebody else," Slocum said.

"It ain't me that's tellin' them. Hell, I'm just a workin' man, same as most folks. But this railroad is gonna be built, whether you like it or I like it. And sure as hell, nobody cares whether no damn Indians like it. That's just the way it is. They call it progress, and it don't come cheap. Somebody's got to pay the price and I'd just as soon it weren't me."

"There will be a lot more trouble before this business is finished," Slocum warned. "You have no idea what trouble is if you think this will all just go away, or that a handful of cavalry can solve the problem."

"Maybe so, John, maybe so. But I'll tell you one thing— I know how it's gonna come out. Maybe not right away, I'll grant you that much. But eventually, it will happen just like I say. I know that for sure, and so do you."

They were close to the camp, now swollen to twice its previous size. Warren Anderson came out of his tent as they reined in. Behind him, a tall, thin young man in uniform with a Lieutenant's bars on his shoulders, brushed his jacket with a handful of thin fingers. He fiddled with his blond mustache which, instead of making him look older, as he obviously had intended, succeeded only in calling attention to just how young he was. Alongside the dark, portly Anderson, he seemed frail as a reed.

Anderson stepped briskly to Slocum's horse, then looked past him for a moment. "Where's Jack Higgins?" he asked.

"Dead," Slocum said, slipping from the saddle. "We buried him out there near where we buried Carlson."

"Redskins got him," Peters said. "A bunch of them jumped us after we finished buryin' Carlson. One white man's grave wasn't enough for 'em, I reckon."

"You get any of them?" Anderson asked.

"No, we . . . unh . . ." Peters started to answer.

"I was asking Slocum," Anderson snapped. "Hold your water, Win."

"Let's go into your tent, Warren," Slocum suggested.

"Good idea." Anderson turned and led the way. The lieutenant followed in his wake, and Slocum brought up the rear.

Once inside, the three men pulled up some camp chairs, and Anderson said, "I guess I should introduce you two before we get started. John Slocum, this is Lieutenant Walter Crum."

Crum extended a slender hand and Slocum shook it, surprised at the strength of the lieutenant's grip.

"Now then, suppose you tell us exactly what happened, John?" Anderson said.

Slocum narrated the story sparingly, trying to touch all the highlights, but downplaying the more sensational aspects of the morning.

Crum nodded his head periodically, as if making mental notes. When Slocum had finished, he said, "You made no attempt to apprehend the woman?"

"No."

"Why not?"

"There was no reason to. She hadn't done anything. She was simply making a trip to her grandfather's burial scaffold. That's not a crime."

"Two white men had been attacked the day before by Sioux Indians. She was a Sioux. It seems simple to me," Crum insisted.

"It's not simple at all, Lieutenant. According to the woman, her grandfather had been shot by Carlson and Chilton without provocation of any kind."

"That's not what Chilton says."

"It's what he *did* say. I told you how he was rambling while he was half unconscious. He said the old man came up to them and started trying to tell them something, then Carlson shot him cold. She says essentially the same thing. Seems to me that has to be what happened. No way she would know what Chilton told me."

"But Chilton was half out of his senses," Anderson said. "You can't hold him to that."

"I can, and I do," Slocum insisted. "He may have changed his story now, but that was after he had a chance to realize what it meant. The truth doesn't reflect any too well on either him or Carlson. He knows that now, and he's trying to make it look better for the two of them."

"You mean," Crum said, "you'd take the word of an Indian woman you don't know from Eve over that of a white man? Is that what you're telling me?"

"That's exactly what I'm telling you, Lieutenant, and that's exactly what I believe. Chilton's story and the woman's story were identical in all important particulars. I think that's significant, and it sure as hell can't be an accident."

"What about Jack Higgins?" Anderson asked.

"What about him?"

"The Sioux killed him. That much you know for sure. You were there, for Christ's sake."

"I don't understand what you're getting at, Warren. What's your point?"

Anderson seemed exasperated. "My point is that hostile Indians attacked and killed one of our men not four hours ago—without provocation."

"I think they'd see it differently. I think the murder of that old man might just seem like provocation to them. And I don't know that I'd blame them. I think if we make a big to-do, it will cause a lot more trouble that we want, or need."

"As long as there are Indians roaming at will across the Powder River country, there will be trouble whether we want it or not, Mr. Slocum," Crum said. He leaned back with a smile of satisfaction, as if he had just closed the argument with an irrefutable point.

"Lieutenant," Slocum asked, "how old are you?"

"I don't see what that has to do with anything."

"Just indulge me for a moment. How old are you?"

"Twenty-three."

"Twenty-three." Slocum nodded as if the answer explained a great deal. In fact, it did just that. "You ever have a command in Indian country before, Lieutenant?"

"No."

"Do you know anything about Indians, not specifically Sioux, but Indians of any kind?"

"Not really."

"Have you ever *seen* an Indian, Lieutenant?"

Feeling safe now, Crum smiled. "Of course. There are lots of them at Fort McAllister. They're there all the time."

"Tame Indians. Peaceable Indians. The kind of Indians the Sioux call Laramie Loafers," Slocum said. "How long since you graduated from West Point, Lieutenant?"

"Three months."

"Three months . . . three goddamned months, and you're going to rid the world of hostile Indians? You're single-handedly going to solve a problem that has been building for seventy years, are you, Lieutenant? You're going to do what no one else has been able to do? And more than likely with a handful of men who spend half their waking hours looking into the open mouth of a whiskey bottle. Men who can't ride, who can't shoot, and who are lucky if they can even read and write. In short, Lieutenant, you and a handful of illiterate buffoons are going to take on ten thousand Sioux warriors and make the Powder River valley safe for the Northern Pacific Railroad. Is that what you're trying to tell me?"

"I don't see why you're being so hostile, Mr. Slocum. I just—"

Slocum didn't let him finish. "Listen, Lieutenant Crum, you ever hear of Captain Fetterman? He had the same ideas you have. He thought he could ride through the whole Sioux nation with seven hundred men. Well, he tried, and he and his whole company were wiped out in a matter of minutes. Lieutenant Grattan thought the same thing, and the same thing happened to him. I'm not being hostile, Lieutenant, not to you *or* the Sioux, because it's in nobody's interest. What I am saying to you is that if you push too hard on this, it will blow up in your face. It will kill you, Lieutenant, and a whole lot of people besides, red and white alike, people who never even heard your name. Now, is that what you want?"

Crum was mad. His pale complexion was turning pink, giving his cheeks a rosy glow and sending plumes of red out from under his tight collar and up under his chin. "What I want, Mister Slocum, is for the men who killed John Carlson and Jack Higgins to be punished for their crime. What I want is for this survey team to be allowed to go about its business without having to look over its shoulder every ten minutes to see whether some damned savage is sneaking up behind it. In short, what I want is to do my job without the likes of you telling me how to go about it. And that is exactly what I *will* do, Mr. Slocum. Whether you like it or not."

"Your job is to keep the peace, Lieutenant, not to make a war. Your job is to see to it that the lid stays on the Powder River valley, which, I think I should point out to you since you seem unaware of it, is Sioux land. Do you understand what I'm saying, Lieutenant? *Sioux* land. Not yours, not mine, and certainly not the Northern Pacific's."

"Now let's all just cool down a minute, everybody," Anderson said. "This is getting out of hand and it ain't going to do nobody any good. I got a survey to do. That's what I care about. I'll do what I have to do to get it done. I think you both make some sense. I think Slocum's right that we don't need to make more of this than it is. But the lieutenant is right, too, John. We can't stand back and do nothing when white men get killed. It gives the redskins ideas. We don't none of us want to see that get out of hand. Nobody'll be safe out here."

"The least you could do, Warren," Slocum said, "is to get the Sioux side of the story. That wouldn't hurt. Even Lieutenant Crum here will have to admit that, I think."

Slocum looked at the officer, waiting for him to object. To his surprise, Crum agreed.

"All right, Mr. Slocum. We'll do that. First thing in the morning, well go find this squaw you have so much faith in. We'll see what happens."

9

Crum was ready at first light. He had marshaled his entire unit, and when Slocum stepped out of his tent, he saw the troopers ready to move. Crum was pacing impatiently back and forth, muttering to a sergeant who was at the head of the line. The sergeant spotted Slocum and said something to Crum, who then spun sharply on his heels.

"It's about time, Slocum," he said. "I thought maybe you had changed your mind and decided to let the army do the dirty work. That's usually the way it is."

"There's no dirty work to be done, Lieutenant. And why the hell do you have so many men? The last thing we need is to go out looking for that woman with twenty armed men. Do you think she'd willingly talk to us under those circumstances?"

Crum puffed out his cheeks, then expelled his breath in one annoyed explosion. "Damn it, Slocum, I'm getting mighty tired of you telling me my business."

"Get used to it, Lieutenant. Until you learn how to do it yourself, somebody sure as hell has to tell you."

"And what should we do, then? Walk across the plains

buck naked with our hands above our heads? Should we leave the guidon here and bring a white flag along? Maybe abject surrender is what will satisfy you and your red friends. Hell, maybe we should *crawl*."

The troopers started to titter, and Slocum glared at them. "Laugh if you want, fellas," he said. "But when Lieutenant Crum gets half of you shot full of arrows because he's too damned stubborn to listen to reason, those of you whose lungs still work won't feel much like it."

Warren Anderson heard the commotion, and swept aside the flap of his tent. "You two still going at it?" he shouted. "Damn it to hell, why don't you just use your heads? John, cut him some slack. Lieutenant, listen to what the man is trying to tell you. You boys are supposed to protect us, not kick a hornet's nest into the middle of camp and beat it with a stick."

Crum glowered, then turned away to converse in a whisper with his sergeant. When he turned back, he said, "All right, I'll take half the men, and leave half here in case there's trouble. But I'm holding Slocum responsible if anything goes wrong."

"Nothing will, as long as you control your temper and use your goddamned head, Lieutenant," Slocum said. He still thought the force too large, but knew that if he argued any harder Crum just might take back the concession he'd already made in order to prove a point. What that point might be was something only Crum would understand, but Slocum thought it best not to push any harder.

"All right with you, Slocum?" Crum asked.

Slocum nodded. "Fine, Mr. Crum. Just fine. I'll get ready."

"Sergeant Conley, pick nine men," Crum bellowed.

The sergeant stood in the stirrups and looked along the line. "Adams, Jeffries, Carter, Bellingham," he shouted,

"Cranshaw, Holderlin, Hitchens, Snopes . . ." He hesitated.

"That's only eight, Sergeant," one of the troopers said.

The sergeant scowled. "I can count, dammit. Who said that?"

One young trooper near the opposite end of the line raised a hand. "I did. Private Hannell, Sergeant. . . ."

"Fine, Hannell, you make nine. That satisfy you?"

"Sure does."

"All right, form up. Column right, by twos," the sergeant hollered. "The rest of you men dismount."

Slocum finished saddling the roan just as the troopers swung right and moved to the edge of the camp.

Crum was on his own mount, his gloves twisted into a mass which he held in one hand and tapped on the palm of the other. "Sergeant Callison, you're in charge."

Slocum swung into the saddle and nudged the roan toward the lieutenant.

Crum nodded, "I'll take the point, Sergeant," he shouted. He turned his horse, a big-shouldered bay, and rode toward the head of the column. Over his shoulder he called, "Mr. Slocum, I'd appreciate it if you'd lead the way along with me."

Slocum rode out thinking that he was following the same route for the third time in three days. Finding the valley was not a problem. Finding the Sioux instead of being found by them would be more difficult. Finding the woman would be the hardest of all. In some ways, it seemed like an impossible task, but he had no choice since it was the only way to avert bloodshed.

As they rode along, the troopers acted for all the world like a bunch of schoolboys on a Sunday ride. Once, Slocum saw a bottle being passed hand to hand, and several of the men taking quick swigs of what was obviously whiskey. For a moment, he thought about calling it to Crum's attention, but decided that he had enough trouble with the lieutenant as it was. The last thing he needed to do was turn the troopers against him, too.

Crum was quiet, almost sullen, as he rode. Slocum tried twice to engage the young officer in conversation, but after the second gruff monosyllable from Crum, he gave it up. He would lead the man, but he wouldn't bother to try to be sociable. It made for a long ride.

When they reached the valley where Carlson had been buried, Slocum rode close to the grave site. The wagon was just as he'd last seen it. The mound of earth, now dry, was sunken in a few spots but otherwise unchanged. Satisfied that no scavengers had gotten to the body, Slocum veered right and started up the slope toward the next valley.

Calling a halt at the top, he used his field glasses to scan the creek bank, tracing the brush from one end of the valley to the other. He pointed out the scaffold and offered his glasses to Crum, who declined. He preferred to use his own spyglass, which he unsheathed from a shiny, new leather case.

"That's the old man's body, you say?"

Slocum nodded. "Yup."

"And you encountered the woman in the creek bed just beyond it?"

"Yeah. About twenty or thirty yards to the left of the scaffold."

"And which way did the Sioux who attacked Higgins go?"

Slocum shook his head. "I don't know. Higgins went that way, out through the mouth of the valley. We were chasing about a dozen warriors on that ridge opposite. They went down the far side and on across to the next valley."

"All right, let's take a look at the scaffold."

Crum nodded to the sergeant, who issued the command,

and Crum led the way down onto the valley floor. Slocum hung back a little, mostly to see what Crum would do. The lieutenant rode close to the scaffold, then stood in the stirrups to get a better look at the body on the platform.

He turned to look for Slocum. "You're sure that's an old man? How the hell can you tell? It's all wrapped up, for Christ's sake."

"Like I said, I unwrapped the buffalo robe. When I climbed down, I saw the woman over there." He pointed toward the brush.

"Let's have a look. Lead the way."

Slocum urged the roan toward the creek. He found a narrow passage through the dense underbrush and eased the horse down into the creek. Crum was right behind him. "She ran upstream," Slocum said. "Cut through the brush— I think mostly to get some cover between herself and me. She didn't know whether I was following her or not."

"They could be anywhere," Crum said. "You should have followed her."

"Easy for you to say, Lieutenant. I didn't know whether she was alone. As it was, I think she was probably with the bunch that tried to decoy us. Add the warriors that jumped Higgins, and you have a pretty fair-sized war party. But if I had to guess, I'd say we should look upstream."

Crum seemed surprised. "Why's that?"

"Because the Sioux almost always camp alongside a stream. They need the water themselves, and they usually have pretty sizable pony herds. It takes care of both if they camp on water."

"Fine, then we'll give it a try. Sergeant?"

"You aren't going to bring the men in here, are you lieutenant?"

"Of course. Why not?"

"Because we're looking for some pretty het-up Indians.

We keep to the creek bottom, we hamper the horses. And there's brush on both sides, with high ground to boot. We could ride right smack into the middle of a thousand warriors, and we'd never know they were there until the arrows started raining down on us."

"I never thought of that." Crum said. He seemed embarrassed to admit it, but he went up a notch in Slocum's estimation for owning up. "What would you suggest?"

"I think we should follow the creek, but stick to the open country, about halfway between the trees and the ridge line. That way, we don't give ourselves away and we leave some room to maneuver, in case we have to. At the same time, it gives us a better chance to spot the village before they know we're here."

Sergeant Conley walked his mount down into the creek, and Crum said, "Sergeant, bring the men on across the creek."

Conley looked confused for a moment, then snapped off a salute that was energetic, if not precise. He wheeled his horse, and moved back through the brush. Slocum walked the roan up out of the streambed, through the brush on the far side of the creek, and out into the open grassland.

Crum stayed behind, waiting for the troopers to make their crossing. When the entire unit joined Slocum, Crum brought up the rear. He said, "How far do you think they are?"

Slocum shook his head. "No idea, Lieutenant. Depends partly on the size of the village. They have to move every few days because the ponies overgraze if they stay in one place too long. A big camp has to move quicker. A small one could stay for weeks. But then there's the Higgins wrinkle. They know somebody'll most likely come looking for them. They could stay where they are hoping to tough it out, or they could scatter to the four winds.'

Crum's expression was one of profound amazement. "You know a lot about the Sioux, do you?"

"Hardly nothing. Most plains Indians have the same habits, though. Their way of life is pretty much the same. Comanche, Kiowa, Cheyenne, Pawnee, you name it. They live off the land. That means limits. And it means they have to respect the land or it won't respect them. Common sense, most of it."

"To you, maybe. But I can guarantee you they didn't teach us this sort of thing at West Point."

"I'm not surprised," Slocum said.

He smiled, but Crum bristled anyway. "You're a southerner, aren't you? By birth, I mean?"

Slocum nodded. "And inclination. . . ."

"Were you in the war?"

"I was, but I don't talk about it."

"I see."

"No, Lieutenant, unless you were there, you don't see anything at all. I hope to God I never see anything like it again. But if you make a mistake in the next few days, I sure as hell will. We all will, and those of us who live through it will regret it."

He clucked to the roan and moved out, leaving the troopers to string along in his wake. He kept to himself, watching the ridges for any sign that they were being observed. He saw nothing to indicate that they were, but he knew that the Sioux were going to be careful, especially once they spotted the bluecoats. The army meant trouble. A small unit usually meant small trouble for the moment, but more often than not, it also meant that a big unit was close by, and that meant big trouble—always.

The terrain grew more vertical as they rode deeper into the Powder River country. The hills were less gentle, less forgiving, and more demanding of both the men and the horses. This was buffalo country, and Slocum kept an eye peeled for signs of the great beasts. The herds were dwindling rapidly under the guns of the hide hunters, and buffalo nearby would almost certainly mean Sioux as well.

It was well after noon when Slocum headed up one more grass-covered slope. The sun was hot, and its glare was harshly insistent. His shoulders ached and his eyes burned, and he wanted to get off his horse and rest, but he wanted to check the next valley first.

As he reached the top of a dome-shaped hill, he slowed, then got off to walk the last thirty-five yards to the crest. He had his Winchester in his hand, and the hill was steep enough so that he used it as a walking stick, bracing the butt on the ground and curling his fingers around the barrel just below the muzzle.

The creek they'd been following snaked around the base of the hill, then doubled back on itself. Far below, a broad bowl of a valley spread out in all directions. The creek meandered back and forth across the floor, bright blue where it reflected the sky, and full of fire where the water broke over stones.

Halfway across the valley, there was a small cluster of Sioux lodges. Their sides were partially rolled up to admit the breeze, and their cone-shaped tops pointed at the sky. There looked to be around one hundred ponies wading in the creek downstream. He'd found them.

Now, all he had to do was get them to talk to him.

10

Lieutenant Crum lay on his stomach, the spyglass glued to his right eye. Slocum lay beside him, watching the village through his C.S.A. field glasses. The village was a small one, only a dozen and a half lodges. If the rule of thumb that normally applied to Sioux villages was valid here, it meant there would be no more than two dozen warriors or so, thirty at the outside. In terms of numbers, it was a disadvantage for the cavalry. Three to one was a long shot, provided all else was equal. But in the continuing struggle between bluecoat and Lakota, little was equal. Crum's troopers were armed with repeating rifles. They had plenty of ammunition, and they were at least familiar with the concept of disciplined maneuvering, even if they were not adept at it.

The Sioux, on the other hand, would be lucky if they had a dozen rifles among them—and most likely, they had fewer than that. The guns they did have would be old breechloaders at best, and probably a couple of muzzle-loading muskets from pre-Civil War days. Their ammunition would be short, and their cartridges short-loaded to save powder, but the real disadvantage under which they labored was their lack of experience in coordinated combat. Each warrior fought on his own. He did what he pleased, and was as interested in demonstrating his bravery to his fellows as he was in defeating the enemy. That was fine when the enemy was the Crow or the Pawnee, people who fought the same way, by the same rules. But bluecoats were different. Sitting Bull knew that and so did Crazy Horse. It was Crazy Horse who had tried more than anyone to make the Sioux understand how important a difference it was. But neither man had much luck so far.

Lying there on the hilltop, Slocum wondered how much of this Lieutenant Crum knew and, if he knew any of it, how much he understood. He hoped the answers were little and none, but it would probably take more than hope to avert a serious incident in the next hour.

"It doesn't look like there are many men down there," Crum whispered. "I've seen a couple of old men, but no young bucks. This might be easier than I thought."

"You aren't going to attack, I hope," Slocum said.

"Of course I am."

"But why? We don't even know whether the woman we are looking for is in this village. And if she is, we certainly don't want anything to happen to her. More than that, it's just plain wrong."

"Slocum, if we go down there and line them up, I would wager a year's wages you wouldn't be able to pick her out of the line—assuming she is there at all."

"Then why attack?"

"What do you expect me to do, man? I'm a soldier. Soldiers fight. That's what they're trained for and that's what they're paid to do."

"To fight enemies, Lieutenant. These people aren't enemies."

"They're Indians, Mr. Slocum," Crum said, collapsing the shiny brass tube of his spyglass and tucking it into its leather case. "That *makes* them enemies."

"For you, maybe, but not for me. Why don't you let me go down there and see what I can find out?"

"Alone?" Crum asked.

"If you're afraid to come with me, I'll go alone, yes. . . ."

"I'm not afraid of a bunch of savages, Slocum. Not the least little bit. But I don't think it's a good idea for you to go down there. You'll just warn them they've been found. That could make things more difficult."

Slocum shook his head in exasperation. "Lieutenant, you just don't get it, do you? If you're right, that there are only a few warriors in the village, then it won't matter whether they know we've found them. On the other hand, if there is a full complement of warriors, then it'll be a whole lot better for everyone if we are as delicate as possible. The woman I met spoke pretty good English. She'd spent some time at one of the forts. The chances are good that this is just a group of Agency Indians on a summer hunt."

"All right, let's say you're right. Let's say I agree that you go down there alone. Suppose the woman is there. Let's even go so far as to say that you get to talk to her. What good does it do?" Crum asked.

"I'm hoping I can convince her to tell her story to someone in a position to do something about what happened."

"Even if her story is true, the man who killed the old redskin is dead. It should be over."

"That's exactly what I'm trying to tell you. But it won't *be* over if people try to use Carlson's death as an excuse to punish the warriors who killed him. By their lights, and frankly, by mine, Carlson got what was coming to him."

Crum shrugged his shoulders. "I think you're crazy. But I'll tell you what I'll do. I'll give you a half hour. You go down to the village and see what you can do. If you get in trouble, we'll try to bail you out, but I don't think that'll do you any good. Your hair would be long gone before we even got on our horses. If the woman is willing to talk, then you signal me and I'll come down and she can tell me whatever it is you think is so important. But at the first sign of trouble, I'm coming down anyway. Please understand that. You may be a goddamned fool, but you're a white fool, and it's my job to protect you, whether you help me or not."

"Thanks, Lieutenant," Slocum said. The irony was lost on Crum, but there was no point in trying to make him aware of it. Getting to his feet, he walked to his horse and opened his saddlebags. Taking out a spare pair of long underwear, he ripped one leg off, slit it along the seam, and opened it into a rough rectangle.

Since there were no trees or brush on the hilltop, he knotted the makeshift flag of truce around his Winchester stock, and swung into the saddle.

Crum stood by watching him. "Slocum," he said, "you're either one of the bravest men I've ever met, or the biggest damn fool on earth. Maybe both."

"That's what I call a lukewarm endorsement, Lieutenant." Kicking the roan, he started toward the valley. Over his shoulder he called, "I'll be back as soon as I can."

He kept his eyes fixed on the village as he walked the roan down the hillside. It was a good two miles to the village, maybe even a little longer, and every yard seemed to tie another one of his nerves into a knot. By the time the land bottomed out, he was wound as tight as a clock. His shoulders were stiff, and it felt like he had a ball of hot lead between his shoulder blades trying to burn its way through his spine.

He was a half mile away by the time he was sure he had been seen. The camp dogs were barking furiously, and several people had come out of the lodges to see what the racket was all about. One of them, an old woman, spotted him, then people started to run from the village toward him.

That convinced him that there were few warriors in the village. A handful of older men and as many boys raced to the pony herd, with bows and lances clutched in their fists. Slocum tried not to break and run. He let the roan keep moving, and raised the rifle high overhead waving it back and forth. He didn't look at the flag, but heard the thick cotton flap every time he changed the rifle's direction.

He watched as the motley crew of defenders thundered toward him, their bows and lances waving, and shield feathers fluttering in the breeze. There was a single pistol shot, but he saw the smoke spew skyward, and turned to make sure Crum hadn't misunderstood. There was no sign of movement on the hilltop, and he allowed himself a deep breath.

Two boys were gradually pulling out in front of the rest of the defenders, their ponies galloping straight toward him. They were yipping and brandishing their bows. Slocum steeled himself as they narrowed the gap. For a moment, it looked as if they were going to charge right into him; their ponies were side by side less than fifty yards away. They thundered on, and Slocum waved the flag frantically.

At the last second, the ponies bumped once, then drifted apart, to pass him on either side. He felt the smack of a bare hand on his left arm, and the tip of a bow grazed his right cheek. He looked back to see the two boys rounding their mounts, grinning from ear to ear as they started back toward him.

An old man was at the head of the rest of the Sioux, and he slowed his war pony. Raising his hand, he brought the defenders to a halt. He barked something in Lakota, and the two boys drifted past Slocum, their expressions hangdog as they looked at the old man, then at Slocum, and then back at the old man. They rode on past and Slocum watched as they took up positions behind the Sioux line, now arrayed in a shallow arc across his path.

The old man, who seemed to be in charge, rode forward until his pony was nose to nose with the roan.

"Do you speak English?" Slocum asked. He rested the rifle, muzzle down, on his thigh, letting the white flag drape over his shoulder.

The chief looked at him without expression for several moments.

"English?" Slocum asked again.

The chief turned to the group behind him. He said something in Lakota, and one of the younger men nudged his pony out of the line and rode up to stop beside the chief.

"I speak English," he said. "What do you want?"

"There is a woman, I don't know her name, and I don't even know if she is in this village, but—"

The young man interrupted. "What do you want with this woman?"

"Her grandfather was killed by two white men. I spoke to her yesterday by her grandfather's scaffold. I want her to tell someone what happened."

"It doesn't matter. The men you speak of are dead. Red Bear is dead. No words will bring him back, or the white men either."

"You're wrong. The man who shot the one you call Red Bear is dead, that is true. But the man with him is not dead, and he says that he never saw Red Bear. He says that he and the dead man were attacked for no reason."

"Lies!"

"I know that. And you know that. But there are other people who do not know that."

"Other white men," the young man said. "But they will not listen to what a Sioux woman says to them. Go away. Leave us alone."

Slocum shook his head. "I can't. Yesterday, another white man was killed, in the same valley where Red Bear lies. There are soldiers who want to come here and punish your people. I know that would be wrong, but . . ."

"We are not afraid of your soldiers. Let them come."

"Your village is small," Slocum said. "You do not have many warriors to defend it. There are women and children who will be hurt if the soldiers come. I know about Sand Creek. I know what happened at the Washita as well as you do. Peaceful Indians, peaceful women, and peaceful children died at those places. Is that what you want to happen here in the valley of the Powder River?"

"I know what happened at the places you mention. And at other places. But no more. That will not happen again. Go away and leave us alone."

"There are soldiers on the hill behind me. Not many, but enough to cause trouble. I have to talk to the woman. I have to get her to talk to the white officer with the bluecoats. He will listen to what she has to say."

"He will listen, but he will not hear. The bluecoat officers are all the same."

Suddenly the line behind the chief and his young companion rippled, then split in half. Slocum glanced past the two men in front of him and saw her.

The young man turned to see what had caused the commotion, and when he saw the woman, he barked at her in her own tongue. She shook her head. He said the same thing, this time pretending to a sternness his years would not permit. Again she shook her head, and responded in Lakota.

The young man looked pained, and he turned back to Slocum. "Gray Fawn says she saw you yesterday. She wants to know why you have come back."

"Tell her."

The young man shook his head.

"Tell her," Slocum barked.

The chief asked the young man what Slocum had said, and when he understood, he issued an order. Glaring at Slocum, the young man used English to explain. Impatient, Slocum interrupted him, and spoke directly to Gray Fawn. "I need you to talk to an officer of the bluecoats, to tell him what happened to your grandfather."

Before she could answer, the line of warriors behind the chief exploded into motion. They raced past the chief and Slocum, and charged toward the hill. Slocum turned in the saddle to see where they were going.

Crum and his troopers were charging down the hill. The two lines closed, and a crackle of gunfire, sounding thin and harmless in the distance, sharply followed the puffs of gray smoke ballooning around the muzzles of the army carbines. Slocum started to turn when something struck him in the back, and he was pulled from the saddle.

He landed hard on his shoulder, and the impact stunned him momentarily. The weight of the young warrior was pinning him to the ground. Slocum tried to throw him off as the troopers thundered down on the village, galloping past him on either side.

Another volley of gunfire exploded as Slocum threw off the weight of his attacker. Scrambling to his feet, he looked for the roan, but it was fifty yards away with its reins gripped tightly in the chief's fist.

Slocum started to run toward the village. "Crum, damn you," he shouted. "What the hell are you doing?"

11

Slocum raced toward Crum, screaming for him to stop. He could see the women and children of the village scattering in every direction. Three or four wounded Sioux lay on the ground, but the casualties seemed light so far.

Crum turned in the saddle as Slocum drew near. The troopers charged their horses toward the village again, firing indiscriminately. Slocum noticed that several of the men were shooting in the air, as if they wanted to make a lot of noise without hiting anyone. He wondered whether those had been Crum's orders, but he wasn't going to wait to find out.

"Looks like we got here just in time to save your ass," Crum shouted. He was grinning like a schoolboy. Slocum launched himself through the air. Crum was still smiling as Slocum slammed into him and knocked him from his horse. The Lieutenant was slender but wiry, and he slipped from Slocum's grasp like an eel. Crum scrambled to his feet and Slocum moved toward him in a crouch. He swung once, catching Crum in the gut and doubling him over.

Crum grunted, "What the hell are you doing?"

Slocum swung again, but Crum ducked away, and the blow glanced off his back as the lieutenant turned sideways.

Something slammed into Slocum's shoulder and he went down to one knee. He turned to see one of the troopers with a rifle poised over his head. As it started to descend, Slocum brought up his arms and turned to try to shield himself from the impact, but the rifle butt hit his forearm first, then cracked against his temple. He fell as if he'd been bludgeoned.

When he came to, his head felt as if it had swollen to twice its normal size. He had a headache that exploded like a load of grapeshot every time he moved, and the pain stabbed in every direction from the center of his skull.

Ignoring the pain, his head wobbled as he shook it to try and clear his vision. Only then did he realize he'd been hog-tied. He was lying on his side, staring at the side of a Sioux lodge that had toppled over. A mound of buffalo robes, utensils, clothing, and food lay beside it, uncovered when the *tipi* had been knocked from its moorings.

He heard someone talking to him, but the words sounded as if they were coming from the bottom of a well. His ears rang and his head swam.

He felt the sharp jab of a boot toe in the small of his back and he turned his head sharply, detonating more grapeshot in his skull. He found himself staring up into the grinning face of Sergeant Conley. "You caught a good one, boy," Conley said. "Lucky you're still alive."

"What the hell is happening," Slocum asked. He wanted the question to be sharp, to crack like a whip, but it sounded thick and almost unintelligible to him.

"We rounded up a few of them redskins is all."

"Why did you attack?"

"Hell, Slocum, you wasn't getting nowhere. Lieutenant Crum, he's a tad impatient. Wants to make a good impression on Phil Sheridan and all, so. . . ." he gave an eloquent shrug.

Slocum swallowed hard trying to dislodge what seemed to be a wad of cotton batting in the back of his throat. "Where's Crum?"

"He'll get to you, soon as he's ready. Meantime, I'd just lay there and wait for them spinnin' stars to go away. You're in deep shit, boy," he said. "Can't say I'm surprised or nothing, neither. Could tell the way you was talkin' that you was an Injun lover."

"You stupid sonofabitch," Slocum said. Even to his own ears it sounded pathetic and impotent. Conley was amused. Then he bent down and grabbed Slocum by the shoulders and hauled him to his feet.

"Might as well take you to the Lieutenant now; save him the trouble of walkin' over here. Course, if it was me, I'd just put a bullet in your head and save us all a whole mess of trouble."

Slocum turned to look at him, ignoring the pain that burned in his shoulders as Conley grabbed his bound arms and shoved them higher on his back. "You don't know what trouble is, Conley, but you're gonna find out now. You can bet on it."

"We'll, I got me a ten spot says you couldn't be more wrong. You got to know how to deal with redskins. The lieutenant don't know so awful much, but he's learnin'. Then again, I reckon I'm a pretty good teacher, so it shouldn't be no surprise."

Slocum shook his head. "You talked him into attacking, didn't you?"

"Hell, man, course I did. You don't think that fool woulda done it on his own, do you? I seen a hundred like him.

They come out here from the East all full of that army horseshit. They don't know what it's like out here. They got big ideas, and they want to make their mark so they can go back home and get a captain's bars, or maybe even a medal, or whatever. Then they go back home and drink wine with fancy ladies, while men like me stay here eating rotten corn and drinking rotgut whiskey. We take the risks and they get all the glory."

"You're a fool, Conley. If you don't get us all killed, I'm going to see to it that you spend a few years in a stockade for what you've done."

Conley grinned broadly. "Last time I looked, you wasn't an officer. Seems to me like I don't have nothing to worry about. Then again . . ." he paused to make his point, "you ain't likely to survive this little affair here. Could be a Sioux'll cut your throat. Maybe an arrow'll get you, maybe a bullet. You never know."

He shoved Slocum so hard he nearly lost his balance, caught himself, then grabbed Slocum by his arms. Once more, flames seemed cauterize Slocum's shoulder joints, and he bit his lip to keep from crying out. Then he saw Crum standing with his hands clasped behind his back. He was pacing back and forth. Beyond him, three dozen Sioux, mostly women and children, were surrounded by the rest of Crum's detachment. The Indians stared at him with faces made of stone. Even the children had overcome their terror, and stood solemnly by their mother's skirts, their hands folded in front of them.

On his next turn, Crum spotted Slocum stumbling along in front of Conley. "Bring him over here, Sergeant," he said.

Conley planted a boot in the small of Slocum's back and shoved him forward. Slocum tripped and fell. Unable to use his hands to break his fall, he twisted to his side. The fall still knocked the breath out of him, and he lay there gasping.

"Get him up, Sergeant," Crum snapped, doing his best impersonation of an officer.

Conley bent over the prostrate Slocum, and once more hauled him up, this time using Slocum's belt. Then he stood behind him, with his fingers still curled through the leather.

Standing at one side of the cluster of women and children, Crum said, "Mr. Slocum, I'd like you to look at the women here. Tell me if you see the woman you spoke to yesterday."

"Why, so you can shoot her?"

Crum laughed. "I'm not a barbarian, Mr. Slocum."

"Then why did you attack a peaceful village?" He glanced past Crum to where three bodies lay, still sprawled where they had fallen, with darkened pools of blood beside them. Gesturing with his chin, Slocum continued. "Did that old woman threaten you, Lieutenant? Was she going to lift your hair? Is that why she's lying there dead?"

"War has its attendant casualties, Mr. Slocum. You're a veteran of the Civil War, and I expect you know that. Your question is disingenuous."

"No, it's not. I'm trying to understand you, Lieutenant; I'm trying to decide how you think—if you think at all. So far, I don't see much evidence that you do."

"I don't really have to justify myself to you, Mr. Slocum. I have a job to do, and I'm trying to do it the best way I know how. Please answer my question. Do you see the woman you told me about?"

Slocum didn't bother to look. There was no way in hell he was going to make things any more difficult for Gray Fawn than they already were. "No, I don't see her," he said.

"Maybe it would help if you looked at them, Slocum," Conley said, jabbing a fist into his back. "Give it a try, anyhow."

Slocum turned, his teeth clenched. "You touch me again, Conley, and I will tear your heart out, do you understand?"

Conley clipped him on the cheek, knocking him to his knees. "Now, you want to tear my heart out, Slocum, you go right ahead and try." He kicked Slocum in the ribs before Crum could stop him.

"That's enough, Sergeant!"

Getting to his knees, Slocum stared at Crum. "Look at yourself, Lieutenant! Damn it, you're no better than Conley. You think you're an officer, and you're behaving like a barbarian. It doesn't matter whether you do anything or not; if you stand by and let Conley make decisions for you, you're no better at all."

He heard footsteps and knew that Conley was getting ready to renew his assault, but Crum stepped past Slocum, and drew his pistol. "I said that's enough, Sergeant. Leave the man alone."

Turning to Slocum, he reached down to help him to his feet. "Mr. Slocum," he said, "you think this woman has information that can explain the attacks on Carlson and Chilton, and on Higgins. I'm prepared to accept that information and act accordingly. But if you won't help me get it, I'll have to go about it some other way. Now, will you help me or not?"

"For Christ's sake, Lieutenant, what the hell's wrong with just asking? Do you have to bully these people to get what you want? There are three dead human beings over there. They had nothing to do with the attack on Johnny Carlson. Why were they killed? How can you justify that, Lieutenant? You say you don't have to justify yourself to me, but somebody judges you—and you damn well better be prepared to justify yourself to whomever that somebody is."

"I don't want a lecture on ethics, Mr. Slocum. What I want is the woman's testimony. Will you identify her or not?"

Slocum shook his head. "No, I won't."

"Then I'll have to get that information some other way— and I intend to stay here until I get it." Crum turned away. "Sergeant Conley, send two men back to Anderson's camp. If we are not back by tomorrow night, I want the rest of the troop brought here to the village the day after. In that event, also tell Anderson to send a courier to Fort McAllister. I want Colonel Roberts to know where we are and what is happening."

"You want reinforcements, Lieutenant?" Conley asked.

"I don't think that will be necessary, but it's up to Colonel Roberts. I think we can keep a lid on things here. More troops might make matters worse."

Conley pulled two troopers from the line, and sent them off. "Bust your asses," he shouted after them. "Don't stop until you get there."

Slocum shook his head in disbelief. "You're making a big mistake, Lieutenant. A very big mistake."

Crum looked at him, and for a moment Slocum saw doubt flit across the lieutenant's features, faint as the shadow of an owl against a new moon. But it was there, and it was the only hope Slocum had.

Shrugging, Crum said, "I'm going to give you one more chance, Mr. Slocum or . . ."

"Or what, Lieutenant. Do you line them up and shoot them all?"

Crum chewed on his lower lip. Shaking his head, he turned his back on Slocum. His hands were clasped behind his back again, and Slocum noticed the fingers twitching almost spasmodically. It seemed as if Crum had no control over them at all, and kept them behind his back to conceal that fact. He whirled suddenly.

"Do you see her, Mr. Slocum?"

Once more Slocum shook his head. "No, I don't."

This time Slocum glanced at the women and children. He saw Gray Fawn staring at him, her eyes bright, but her face as impassive as the others. Slocum cast his eyes down to avoid giving her away. He realized that Crum had forgotten that there were warriors in this village, and that they would be coming back. If they arrived after nightfall, or the next day, or any time before the rest of the troopers arrived, it could be a bloodbath. If they arrived later than the reinforcements, it would definitely be one. There was a better than even chance that word of the attack on this village was already spreading. It was possible, even likely, that the Sioux would rally warriors from other villages. Slocum sucked in a breath and held it, knowing that no matter what happened, it was unlikely he would live another week.

Crum had resumed his pacing in front of the prisoners.

Suddenly, Gray Fawn stepped out of the crowd. "I am the woman you look for," she said.

12

Slocum lay on the floor of a Sioux lodge. The softness of the buffalo robes lulled him a little. He was exhausted, and the urge to sleep was overwhelming. But he knew that he couldn't afford to sleep—not yet, at least.

Gray Fawn was across from him. Like him, her arms were tied behind her back, and she had her ankles bound as well.

Outside, he could hear the raucous sounds of the troopers as they passed a bottle around, and then probably another. Their voices were growing louder, and their speech slurred as they celebrated a victory Slocum couldn't understand.

He was angry—angry enough to want to kill. He swore to himself that if he managed to get loose, he would kill, and Sergeant James Conley would be the first one to die. There might be others, but Conley would be enough.

In the gloom of the lodge, he could barely make out Gray Fawn's shape where she lay against the wall curled in a ball. He wanted to talk to her, but he had no idea whether a guard had been posted outside the lodge, and he couldn't take the risk of being overheard.

Stretching out to his full length, he started to roll across the lodge floor. Despite the cushioning of the robes, every time he landed on his shoulders pain shot the length of his arms. His head throbbed, and he was conscious of a knot the size of a hen's egg on the side of his skull. With every stab of pain, he made another mental note to get even with James Conley.

Crum was beneath contempt. He'd allowed himself to be manipulated by a barbarian, and there was no room in Slocum's heart for sympathy for the lieutenant. He didn't wish Crum ill, but he knew that if the lieutenant were to pay a high price for his stupidity, it would be difficult, if not impossible, to dampen an eye on his account.

Halfway across the lodge floor, he rolled over several stones that took him by surprise, then he realized they were used to contain the fire that normally burned in its center. Maneuvering was difficult, and rather than change direction, he gritted his teeth and rolled out of the fireplace and onto the softness of more buffalo skins.

Gray Fawn said nothing as he approached, and he wondered whether she was even awake. It wasn't that late, just an hour or so past sundown, but he knew how tempted he was to let his mind drift off in the fog of sleep. He wouldn't have blamed the woman if she had succumbed to the same temptation.

He sensed that she was close and paused in his painful movement to whisper, "Gray Fawn?"

She didn't answer. He thought she might be sleeping after all, and tried again, raising his voice just a little. "Are you awake? Gray Fawn?"

Still no answer. He rolled closer, and suddenly he could feel her body against his. His back was to her, and the soft buckskin of her dress brushed against his outstretched fingertips.

Beneath the deerskin, he could feel the curve of her hip. He tapped his fingers lightly, then a little harder, trying to waken her. She continued to be silent. Her breathing was deep and regular. He was almost certain she was asleep.

He sat up with some difficulty, got to his knees with even more, then fell forward on his stomach, so he could bring his mouth close to her ear. Wisps of hair tickled his nose as he leaned close, and he remembered how black and shiny her hair was. She smelled like flowers, he thought— no, not flowers—a flower. It reminded him of honeysuckle, the same vine that had nearly buried his grandmother's cottage with its thick leaves and aggressive tendrils. He remembered the bees swarming around the cottage all summer long. He wondered whether honeysuckle grew here in the Powder River country, and could not recall ever having seen any.

For a moment, he thought he should let the woman sleep. She was bound every bit as securely as he was, that much he knew. There wasn't really much she could do even if she were to awaken. He felt sorry for her; she had lost a close relative, and then had seen her village attacked. For all he knew, she may have lost someone else close in that attack. Then, for reasons he didn't quite understand, she had taken the substantial risk of identifying herself to Crum when Slocum himself had refused to do so. He didn't know why she had done it, but he felt a wave of tenderness for her, and more than a little admiration for her courage.

That she was achingly beautiful made it all the more painful to lie there beside her, trussed up like a Christmas turkey. Without even thinking about it, he leaned a little closer, pursed his lips, and kissed the lobe of her ear. Then he lay down and turned his face away.

"Why did you do that?" she whispered. She sounded annoyed with him.

He was taken by surprise. "I thought you were asleep. I just . . ."

"Why did you do that?" she asked again, her voice a sibilant hiss in the darkness.

"Why did I do what?"

"Just now, to my ear. Why did you do it?"

Slocum was embarrassed. "I don't know," he stammered. "I just . . . I thought . . . I don't know."

"You are frightened for me, aren't you? You are afraid something bad will happen."

"Yes."

He heard movement as she shifted her body. "I am frightened for you, too."

"Why did you tell them who you are? You shouldn't have said anything. They never would have known. I'm the only one who saw you."

"It doesn't matter. Nothing matters anymore. Nothing that happens can change things."

"That's not true. It does matter, and it will continue to, until we make them pay for what they've done."

"That will never happen. White men always get away with killing Indians, even old ones, women, and children. You are a white man, you should know that."

It was Slocum's turn to be annoyed now. "Not all white men are bad."

"I have yet to meet the first who isn't," she whispered. Her voice, despite the whisper, was harsh, and full of pain and acid. She was silent then, and the silence dragged on for a long time. When she spoke again, her voice had softened. "I'm sorry," she said, "I shouldn't have said that. I know that what you did was very brave. I am just sorry that it will not change anything that happens. Or anything that has already happened."

"I'm not dead yet," Slocum said. "I'll think of something.

There has to be some way out of this mess."

"When my brother returns, there will be trouble."

"Your brother?"

"Yes. He is out hunting. Almost all the young men are. But they will come back soon. Then there will be trouble. We are . . . what do you say . . . hostages? And that will make it difficult, but the young men will not . . ." She seemed to have fallen permanently silent, but then continued. "Maybe he will not come back. Maybe he will go to our village. Then—"

The entrance flap of the lodge was pulled aside abruptly, and flickering light flooded into the darkness. Slocum rolled onto his back to see who had entered.

Lieutenant Crum stood there with a burning brand in his hand. "Slocum?" he called. "Where are you?"

"Here," Slocum said, sitting up. "You know what a big mistake this is, Crum. Why don't you stop before matters get out of hand?"

"Not now, Slocum. Not now. I just wanted to make sure you were holding up all right."

"Why do I have to hold up, as you put it, at all? Why does Gray Fawn—"

"Is that her name? That's almost poetic, isn't it? It's amazing that savages like these could—"

"Damn you, Crum, when are you going to wake up? The Sioux are not savages, they're people, just like you and me. In fact, I think they're probably better than either of us. Why don't you arrest Conley, for Christ's sake? He's the one who ought to be tied up."

"I wish you'd reconsider, Slocum."

"Reconsider what?"

"If you were to be more cooperative, I could release you. As it is, I think you're too involved. I don't think you're seeing things clearly. We'll talk again in the morning. Think about what I said."

With that, Crum turned and ducked out through the entrance flap, leaving the lodge darker than before he'd entered.

"We have to get out of here," Slocum whispered. "I don't trust him, and I sure as hell don't trust Conley."

"Conley," she whispered, "is that the man who was beating you?"

"Yeah."

"Why did he do that?"

"It's a long story, Gray Fawn. There's no time to tell it now."

"This is my uncle's lodge," she said. "They didn't search it before they put us in here."

"Does that mean there's something we can use—a knife maybe?"

"Yes. My uncle, Long Bow, always keeps a knife by his sleeping robes. During the day, his wife hides it so the children won't find it."

"Do you know where?"

"No. But I know it is in here somewhere."

"Great," Slocum said, "that's just great. We need it to cut ourselves free, but we can't look for it *unless* we're cut loose. Don't you have any idea where it might be?"

"No. We'll have to search the robes, that's all. It has a thick bone handle, so I think we might feel it. We'll have to try."

Slocum gave a sigh of exasperation. "All right," he said. "You check one half of the lodge and I'll check the other. If you find anything, don't call out, just come to me. I'll do the same."

He rolled away from her, and suddenly felt very much alone. It was as if her closeness had comforted him somehow. He tried not to think about the scent of her, or the feel of her buckskin dress against his fingertips.

Crossing the fire pit once more, the stones dug into his back and sides, but he ignored the pain and continued to roll across the floor to the far wall of the lodge. In the darkness, it was going to be difficult to tell if he had covered every square inch. He felt like a blind man, as if his eyes were suddenly useless grapes or balls of jelly in a bone box, useful for nothing at all.

Using his hands was going to be too time consuming, and with the weight of his body pressing down on them, he could barely move them anyway, so he decided to use his calves wherever possible. Any hardness under the robes, any lump that seemed out of place, he could check with his fingers.

He felt like a fool, lying on his back and letting the backs of his legs slide across the thick fur of the buffalo skins. He kept teasing himself, thinking he'd found something, only to learn, after painful contortions, that he had imagined it. Inch by inch, he pressed his calves against the ground. He lifted his legs, moved them an inch, then let them down again.

He could hear the whisper of Gray Fawn's skin against the soft leather of her dress each time she lifted her legs to move. The sound summoned images of those legs that he couldn't keep out of his mind. He wondered what it would be like to slip the dress over her head, and to feel her skin with his fingertips. But the thoughts made for painful pressure in his jeans, and he tried to brush them away.

It had been nearly two hours, and he was almost back to the fire pit. The raucous noise of the troopers had subsided, and he thought with disgust that they were either stupefied or sleeping. As near as he could figure, it was about midnight. He pressed on for another fifteen minutes, or so.

Maneuvering around the fire pit, he realized he still had

another quadrant to cover, and he knew he would never make it. He heard footsteps outside, as if someone were walking around the lodge. He realized that Conley could step into the tipi at any moment and put a bullet in his brain or slit his throat.

Then he heard another noise, much closer. He turned in that direction just as something bumped against him. He felt the softness of her breasts press down on his chest as Gray Fawn leaned over him. "I've got it," she said. "I've got the knife!"

13

"Give it to me!" Slocum whispered. "Quickly!"

Gray Fawn lay beside him and turned her back. He groped with his hands, shifted his body a bit, and felt the ropes around her wrists. Turning his shoulder to get his hands in position, he felt the cold bone of the knife handle. It seemed to have been elaborately carved, and his fingers groped to get a firm grip.

"Do you have it?" she hissed.

"Not yet. Wait." Curling his fingers around the handle, he pushed toward her a bit. Then he squeezed the handle and said, "There, I've got it."

Now that he had the knife, he wasn't sure what to do with it. There was no way he could manipulate the blade with enough precision or enough force to slice through the heavy cords binding either of their hands; at least not without risking a slashed wrist.

"Wait," she said. "There's a cover on the blade."

"Maybe I can shake it off."

"No, it's tied with rawhide. Roll onto your stomach and just hold it still."

Slocum did as he was told. Once more, he heard the footsteps outside the lodge. They were heavier now, sounding more determined, as if someone outside were trying to make up his mind about something, pacing back and forth, circling the lodge now and then, trying to work up his nerve. He wondered for a moment if it was Lieutenant Crum trying to decide whether or not to turn him loose, but that seemed too optimistic by half. He considered it only because he wanted it to be true. It wasn't, and somewhere deep inside him, he knew it. Then the specter of Conley forced its way into his consciousness. Maybe it was the sergeant trying to get up enough courage to come inside and kill them both. That was more like it, and he tried not to think about it. The footsteps were making him nervous.

He lay still, the knife held as securely as he could hold it, and heard Gray Fawn shift her position. She seemed to be struggling with something, and he realized she was getting to her knees.

"What are you doing?" he whispered.

"Shush, be still."

A moment later, he felt a tickle as she draped her hair across his wrists and fingers. Then he realized what Gray Fawn was trying to do. She was going to untie the rawhide with her teeth. It was risky, because her saliva could swell the rawhide and make it tighter, but there was no alternative.

The constant teasing of her hair made it difficult for him to hold onto the knife, and he was forced to bite his lower lip to distract himself from the tickling sensation. He heard a series of sharp clicks as her teeth kept slipping from the rawhide. Each time she lost her grip, she puffed her breath out in exasperation.

"Hurry," he hissed. "Hurry up!"

She was too busy to answer him. Again and again her

teeth slipped and finally she said, "It's no good. I can't do it. I'll have to bite through it."

"Do it, then," Slocum urged.

Now he felt the steady rhythm of her jaws working. She kept pressure on the rawhide thong, working her teeth from side to side. Suddenly, the pressure vanished, and she sighed in relief.

"It's off," she said. "Hold still."

There was a soft sound as she gripped the sheath between her clenched teeth and backed away. The knife handle almost slipped from his grasp, and then he felt the slap of the sheath on the back of his thighs as she let go.

"There," she whispered. "It's off."

Now, all he had to do was figure out how to take advantage of the blade without slashing either one of them. There was only one way to do it. He rolled over onto his back, holding the knife firmly in both hands. He felt the sharp prick of the blade as it sliced through his shirt and opened a small cut on his lower back. Raising himself to a sitting position, he brought the knife down as hard as he could, driving its point through the buffalo robes under him and into the dirt beneath them.

Sliding his hands down along the bone grip, he searched for the cutting edge of the blade. When he found it, he rotated to the left, as if the knife were a pivot. When the edge of the blade faced away from him, he whispered, "Sit down with your back to me. I'll hold the knife. You'll have to cut your own ropes while I keep the knife steady. Be careful, the blade is razor sharp."

She didn't answer, but immediately swung her body around as he had instructed. She leaned back against him, then scooted back until she could rest the ropes against the blade. Working her hands up and down, she sawed away at the cords. Slocum could feel her shoulder blades against his back, and the play of her muscles under her buckskin dress. He found himself once more thinking about her body, trying to imagine feeling those muscles with the flat of his hand. Once more, he felt a stirring for which the time and the place were both inappropriate.

He heard one of the strands of the ropes part with a pop, then another, and then a third. The ropes were thick, and it would take some time for her to cut all the way through them.

He was struggling to hold the blade in position because the edge of knife kept turning away from the pressure of the ropes. His fingers were cramping, and his shoulders ached. Another strand parted, and then one more.

Finally, he felt Gray Fawn flex her shoulders, and suddenly her arms were no longer between them. She got to her knees and leaned over his shoulder. Once more, the scent of honeysuckle swirled around him as she leaned close to whisper, "I'll take the knife now."

He relaxed, and heard the scrape of the blade as she yanked it from the ground. Then he felt the cold tingle of the steel as she slipped the blade between his wrists and sliced through the ropes. When his hands were free, he rubbed his wrists to restore circulation while Gray Fawn cut the cords binding her legs.

Handing him the knife, she waited until he freed his own legs. "What now?" she whispered.

"I don't . . . shush. . . ."

Again the footsteps had scraped by outside. Glancing at the entrance flap, he noticed a thin line of light. The flap itself seemed to glow, and he realized that there was probably a large fire in the center of the camp. A shadow drifted past the glowing flap, momentarily darkening the outline of the firelight.

"Lie down like you're still tied up," Slocum hissed.

He lay on his back, groping desperately for the knife, but it eluded his grasp.

Suddenly, the flap was jerked aside. Someone stooped to enter, but he was silhouetted by the fire outside, and it was not possible to see who it was. He could hear the man's heavy breathing. Whoever it was bent to come inside, lost his balance, and fell in a heap, while cursing under his breath. It was obvious he was drunk.

Getting to his knees, with the entrance flap now draped across his back, the man crawled inside, mumbling to himself. Slocum continued to pat the long fur of the buffalo skins all around him. Where the hell was the knife, he wondered.

It grew dark again as the man made it all the way inside and the flap fell back into place. Slocum could hear the scrape of rough cloth as it was dragged over the buffalo hides. The man was crawling on his hands and knees, and still mumbling. As he came closer, Slocum could make out the words. "Where the hell are you, darlin'? Come to papa. Papa gonna show you a good time, honey. A *good* ole time."

The man stopped talking to himself, and once more there came the scrape of cloth. Metal clinked once, and then again. It sounded like coins in a pocket, and Slocum realized the intruder was looking for something.

A sharp pop was followed by the rush of a match igniting. Flame mushroomed in the air in the middle of the lodge, then it flickered down until it almost went out. The bluish light, little more than a pinpoint, rose and fell as the flame tried to catch. Then it started to balloon as the acrid stench of phosphorus filled the tipi.

Slocum could see the trooper now; his shirt was open, and his face was flushed. His eyes opened and closed quickly, their rheumy glaze catching the light which gave them the look of iridescent marbles. A swirl of sour alcohol drifted past Slocum as his fingers found the cold steel of the blade. They crept along it and finally curled around the bone handle of the knife.

The trooper, Private Hannell, teetered precariously on his knees as he peered under the match flame, which flared suddenly. Hannell cursed as the match burned his fingers before it went out.

Slocum moved then, trying to freeze the drunken trooper's location in his mind. On his feet, he heard the trooper mutter, "Whaaathehell's goin' on?"

A second match grated and popped, then burst into flame and Slocum sprang. His angle was slightly off, but there was no time to adjust. He hurtled by, narrowly missing the trooper and sending the newly lit match to the buffalo robes where it guttered out, adding the stench of singed hair to the air.

Still gripping the knife, Slocum turned and reached out, trying to find the trooper. He felt cloth under his hands and dug his fingers into the flesh beneath it. Hannell yelped in pain. Tugging, he jerked the man over, and heard him land with a thud, then he dove on him.

Hannell started to yell as Slocum clamped his hand over the trooper's mouth. Teeth sank into the flesh of his palm, and Slocum lashed out with the knife handle. He felt it strike flesh, then bone, and the trooper groaned as he tried to roll away. Slocum twisted away, and Hannell's teeth released their hold on his hand. Keeping his hand in place, Slocum felt the man struggling to breath. He pinched his nose closed, listening to the thud of Hannell's boots on the skin-softened floor of the lodge. The drumming lasted a few seconds, and the man lay suddenly still.

Slocum could hear his own hoarse breathing. He removed his hand, then shook it to try to ease the pain. Patting the trooper's body, he found the man's holster. He opened the flap and pulled out a revolver, which he stuck in his belt. On the opposite hip, he found an ammunition pouch, tore it loose, and stuffed it into his shirt. In the dark, he ran his hands over the trooper's face. Hannell had an ugly lump on his left temple where the knife handle had struck him, but he was breathing.

"Gray Fawn," Slocum hissed. "Where are you?"

"Here," she answered. He moved forward, one hand extended toward the sound. It brushed the buckskin over her hip. Glancing at the glow around the entrance flap, he pushed the woman in the opposite direction. Then he followed her, nearly losing his balance as he stepped on the shinbone of the unconscious trooper. Regaining his balance, he bumped into Gray Fawn, then slipped past her, reaching out to grab her arm and pull her after him. Using the knife, he quickly sliced through the skin of the lodge, first vertically, then horizontally. Pushing aside one of the triangular flaps the cuts had made, he peered out. He could see several lodges, but nothing else.

There was probably a sentry or two posted, but from the sounds of the revelry earlier, there was the chance that even the guards had had too much to drink.

"Follow me," he whispered, then pushed through the gaping hole on his hands and knees. Turning, he watched Gray Fawn slip through the opening and clamber to her feet.

Holding a finger to his lips, he pointed to the next lodge, then signaled that she should get behind it while he made sure they weren't discovered. He watched her dart away for a split second, then moved left to peer past the side of the lodge. The fire flickered, the timber crackled and popped once, sending sparks dancing on the heated air before they winked out.

Looking back over his shoulder, he could no longer see

the woman. It was time to go. He turned and sprinted for the lodge, rounded it, and found Gray Fawn crouched behind it. Taking her by the hand, he pulled her into a fast shuffle, and headed out into the open meadow behind the camp. The firelight barely reached that far, and as they ran, they left it even further behind.

Off in the distance, a horse nickered, then another, and two more.

He headed for the trees, conscious that Gray Fawn was keeping up with him, and that they had to get away from the camp before somebody missed Hannell and raised the alarm. He ran on tiptoe, trying to muffle the sound of his footfalls. The tall grass swished and slashed at his pantlegs, surrendering swarms of insects that clouded around him, their buzzing angry in his ears. On every side, crickets chirped, but stopped as he passed near, then started up again behind him. The deeper he ran into the grass, the louder they sounded, and soon it was all he heard.

He ran nearly half a mile before slowing, then sank to his knees. Gray Fawn stood beside him, her hands were on her hips and she was bending at the waist. She reached out and rested one hand on his shoulder to support herself, and he looked up at her.

Leaning close, she pressed her lips against his ear, then pulled back, smiling. "Where are we going?" she asked.

Slocum shook his head. He didn't have the faintest idea.

14

They were climbing a hill behind the village. Slocum stopped fifty yards from the top and looked back down on the scene below. Two men approached the fire with their arms full of wood. One man dumped his load into the flames, and a cyclone of smoke and sparks twirled up into the sky. The other let the logs in his grasp fall to the ground a few feet away.

They were the only people moving in the small camp. While he watched, they backed away from the fire and sank back into the shadows from which they'd come. Far across the valley, a sliver of moon hung low in the sky. Its light was just enough to cast long shadows ahead of the trees looking like slender fingers of charcoal against the silver-gray grass.

"We need help," Slocum said, "and to get help, we need horses."

"There is another village, but it is a long way, too long to walk, and I am so tired," Gray Fawn said "But if we can get to it, we can get help."

"What kind of help? I don't want to start a war. I want to stop one."

"Do you think if you bring soldiers, it would be any different? You brought these soldiers, and you see what happened."

He nodded. She was right, but he didn't know what to do. He knew that the rest of Crum's troops would arrive in two days, probably late, but it still didn't give them much time to avert an all-out confrontation. Once the troops reached the Sioux village, it would be difficult to dislodge them without heavy casualties on both sides.

"All right," he said, "take me to the village."

She looked at him for a long moment, as if trying to decide whether she could trust him or not. He didn't blame her for her uncertainty. The best intentions seemed to blow up in his face. She must realize that, he thought. He sighed.

"Your brother, when will he return?" he asked.

She shrugged. "Tomorrow, the next day. Maybe longer."

"Do you know how to find him?"

She shook her head. "No. The country is big and the buffalo are scarce. Besides, he might not come back here. He might go to the village of Two Elks." She stood up and started to walk toward the hilltop. Slocum got wearily to his feet and trudged after her. She moved easily, despite her own weariness, as if walking uphill were something she did for enjoyment, her hips rocking smoothly with every step.

Crossing the hilltop, they started down toward a patch of cottonwoods. The slope was steep and the grass hampered him as he walked. The angle of the slope made walking in his boots almost painful because of their high heels. Gray Fawn looked back at him. She realized his problem at once. "Take off your boots," she said. "It will make it easier for you to walk."

Slocum nodded, then sat down on a ground swell and tugged off his boots. He looked at the copse below and saw the band of silver water snaking among the trees. The moon was sinking, and it would be dark in a little more than an hour. He kept thinking about the village, and about the sentries. There might be only two of them, and chances are they had had as much to drink as the others. They would be tired and, more than likely, a little careless.

"I have an idea," he said. She strode back uphill toward him, and stood over him with her arms crossed.

"What is it?"

"We might be able to get horses after all. Those guards are not going to be too careful, and we might be able to slip up on the herd from the other side."

"And if they are careful, and they hear us, then what?" she asked.

"They'll never chase us in the dark. So we're no worse off than we are now," Slocum answered.

"But we lose time, and they might take out their anger on the others."

"I don't think so. I think they're scared and—"

"And drunk, and stupid and . . . white."

"It's our best chance, Gray Fawn. Trust me."

She cocked her head toward the sky, either debating whether to trust him or gauging the remaining moonlight; he wasn't sure. He hoped it was the latter.

"All right, I'll trust you," she said. She reached down to take him by the hand, and helped him to his feet. He pinched the uppers of his boots in the fingers of his left hand and followed her downhill.

"Why are we going this way?" he asked.

"You'll see," she said. "If I am to trust you, then you have to trust me, too."

They entered the cottonwood stand, and the earth turned to dark gray and silver beneath them. He could hear the gurgling of the creek up ahead, and the whisper of cottonwood leaves as a cool breeze hissed through them.

He looked back over his shoulder, but could no longer see the moon. The grass among the trees was shorter, and it felt cool under his feet. His socks were soaked with dew, and little beads of moisture glittered among the blades.

He could see the creek now, its dull sheen like newly polished pewter in the pale moonlight. Only then did he realize how hungry and thirsty he was. He wanted to run and hurl himself into the creek; to lie on his back and let the cool water wash away the aches and pains, and soak up its cleansing energy.

The bank of the creek was marked by lush grass and a band of sand right along the water's edge. Gray Fawn tugged his hand, pulling him toward the creek. There was a strength in her that belied the apparent frailness of her body.

She turned downstream, still tugging him in her wake. She was moving faster, as if she had some particular destination in mind. "Where are we going?" he asked. He'd meant to whisper, but his voice seemed loud, almost petulant in the silence.

She shook her head as if to tell him not to ask. The creek widened out then, its water suddenly placid where it flowed into a deep pool. Thirty yards ahead, he could see a ridge of foam. The dull roar of water tumbling over a wall of rock filled the glade with its soft, but incessant thunder.

Letting go of his hand, she sat down on the grass and pulled off her moccasins. Getting to her feet again, she bent, grabbed the hem of her buckskin dress and tugged it up over her head. Then, she let it fall to the ground.

"What are . . . ?" but he stopped. She stood there facing away from him, the prominent curve of her hips glistening with moonlight, and the small of her back was a pool of silver for a moment. She turned slightly as she stepped toward the water's edge, revealing the heavy curve of one full breast. It gleamed with moonlight for a moment as she raised one leg, stepped into the water, and sank to her hips.

Stunned both by her beauty and by the suddenness of her action, Slocum sat there with his jaw slack. She dove forward, her body arching, her perfect ass sparkling for a moment, before disappearing under a sheet of pale silver fire as the water surged up around her. She swam the width of the pool, her arms working smoothly, trailing veils of water with every stroke. Reaching the far side, she stood up near the bank, the water coming only to mid-thigh. She turned to face him then, water streaming over her skin, and the dark patch between her legs studded with a hundred jewels. Her full breasts were firm, their nipples pert and prominent.

She shook her head, her braids lashing like black whips and spraying water in every direction, scattering drops across the pond and sending a thousand ripples over its surface.

She started to walk toward him, the water rose slowly up her body, covering her thighs, then the triangle of coal black hair, then the slight mound of her stomach and up toward her magnificent breasts. Then, she launched herself gliding like a water snake, with just her face above the surface, sending a vee trailing off on either side of her.

Slocum tugged off his socks, then his shirt, and jeans, and dove into the pond. He swam toward her, but she shook her head. Holding a finger to her lips, she said, "Sssshh!"

He stopped, standing now in water up to his shoulders. Gray Fawn swam past him, heading toward the center of the pool. He saw her take a deep breath, and dive beneath the surface with her legs suddenly slicing through the water. Then she disappeared altogether. She reappeared a few moments later, shook the water from her hair, then took another deep breath, and disappeared once more.

This time she stayed down longer, then she shot to the surface and raised a hand high over her head. Flapping and twisting, a trout tried to free itself from her grasp, but she had two fingers hooked through one of its gills. Treading water, Gray Fawn pulled herself toward the bank with one hand, and kept a tight grip on the wriggling fish with the other.

In shallow water once more, she stood to walk the last fifteen feet, then climbed out and tossed the trout far back onto the grass. Slocum swam toward her, reaching the bank and climbing out as she bent to retrieve her dress. He put a hand on her hip as she straightened up. She flinched, but made no attempt to get away.

He let his hand rest on her cool, smooth skin for a moment, then she turned to him with her dress clutched in one hand. She shook her head, but said nothing, then raised the dress over her head. With her arms extended, the lushness of her body was overwhelming. She slipped the bunched buckskin over her head, and tugged it down to her shoulders. Her arms snaked through the sleeves, and then she shimmied to let gravity pull the dress over her sleek skin. He noticed her dark aureoles, pebbled by the cool breeze, as well as the fullness of her breasts and the stiffness of her nipples. Gently, he reached out and cupped her breasts in his hands until the buckskin brushed his trembling hands aside, leaving them to fumble in the air.

She stood there for a long time, looking at him but saying nothing. Glancing down, she smiled then reached out with one hand, and traced the length of his erection with a solitary fingernail. She closed her hand over its firmness for an instant, stopping its quiver for a split second. Then she let it slide away from the warmth of her touch as she backed up a step, turned and walked away.

Slocum turned back to the creek, took two steps and dove into the pool. He was embarrassed now, both at his nakedness, and at the futility of his gesture. Swimming across the pool, he climbed out on the far side and sat in the grass. The breeze chilled him, but he couldn't bring himself to cross over again. Not yet.

He could just make out Gray Fawn crouching at the edge of the grass. The beige of her dress and the blackness of her hair blended in with the mix of moonlight and shadow under the cottonwoods. He watched as she straightened up, went to his clothes, and gathered them. Then she walked to the wall of rock and tiptoed across it with the water foaming around her slender ankles.

She glided toward him, her eyes fixed on his face, and his clothing bunched against her stomach. When she was right in front of him, she let the clothing fall, and reached out with one hand to once more pull him to his feet.

She looked him up and down, then extended one delicate hand and used a finger to follow the path of a scar that arched across his chest. Withdrawing her hand, she smiled. She glanced once more at his waist, and the smile broadened.

"I've cleaned the fish," she said. "We need to eat if we are going to help my people."

"Where did you learn to do that? With the fish, I mean."

"My grandfather taught me," she said. Turning away from him, she started to sob, and he was sorry that he had reminded her of such a painful loss. Her shoulders shook, and she buried her face in her hands. He felt impotent and foolish. Not knowing what to do, he stepped toward her, wrapped his arms around her, and pulled her close.

She made no move to pull away. Instead, she seemed to collapse toward him, hunching her shoulders. She turned around without breaking his embrace. Her body molded itself to his then, with only the softness of the deerskin between them. Laying her head on his shoulder, she said, "I miss him so much."

Her arms circled his waist, with her hands resting on the curve of his cheeks. They were perfectly still, but he had never felt anything in his life more erotic.

He felt himself stirring. She felt it too, and switched her hips, snuggling in still closer. Tilting her head back, she stood on tiptoe, kissed him chastely on the cheek, and said, "We should eat now. The moon is almost down. We'll have to leave soon."

He nodded, then bent to kiss the top of her head. "All right," he said.

15

Slocum choked down the raw fish. At first it felt slimy, and he had to repress the impulse to gag on the chewy flesh. But the juice refreshed him, and after a few tentative bites his hunger took over, and he wolfed down several strips of the cold trout.

When he was finished eating, Gray Fawn pointed to the sky. "The moon is gone," she said. "It is time to go."

They followed the creek. Since he had the stolen Colt revolver, he gave Gray Fawn the knife. She moved silently, almost wraithlike. She was just a shadow along the creekbank now that the light was gone, and she could barely be seen. Her footsteps were so silent that he strained to hear them. If he hadn't known she was just a few paces ahead of him, he doubted if he would have heard her at all.

The creek burbled on their left, and he kept peering ahead, leaning forward to see where to place his feet. He was afraid that one careless step could give them away, even though the village was more than two miles downstream. He wanted to get in the habit of walking furtively— a habit that his life might depend on once they drew closer.

Gray Fawn knew the layout of the village, and had insisted they follow the stream because it rounded the steep hill behind the village and would lead them to the broad meadow where the Sioux ponies grazed at night. It seemed likely that the sentries would be more concerned with the security of the camp itself. Unlike the Indians they held captive, their lives did not depend on a herd of ponies, and Slocum was banking on their lack of attention.

Conley was the only one of the ten troopers who had much experience on the frontier, but since he was one of the more avid drinkers, it was probable that he would be sleeping off a night's whiskey. Crum struck Slocum as upright and probably a teetotaler, but he was too much the West Pointer to sit up all night watching a herd of ponies.

Suddenly a hill loomed up ahead; a massive shadow Slocum could see through the thinning cottonwoods. He knew that the village lay just beyond it and he increased his pace a bit to catch up to Gray Fawn. He failed to see her in time and nearly knocked her down when he bumped into her.

"When we get there," Slocum said, "you stay back and let me get the horses."

"I can do it better than you," she whispered. "You make too much noise."

"I have a gun."

"That makes more noise than you do. Even a drunkard would hear it. If we hope to get away, then it is best if I get the horses."

Slocum knew she was right, but his pride wouldn't let him agree. "We'll both go," he suggested.

She seemed to expect him to offer such a compromise, and agreed to it after pausing long enough to let him know that she wasn't entirely pleased with the idea.

They moved slowly now, conscious that a false step might wake one of the dogs or, worse yet, one of the troopers. After another fifty yards, the stream curled to the right, rounding the base of the hill. The trees were all but gone now, replaced by a ten-yard band of brush on either bank of the creek. In some places it grew almost to the water's edge and they had to step into the creek to avoid it. As they neared the village, the brush thinned out and then disappeared, leaving a broad, sandy stretch of ground between the water's edge and the meadow.

Then, the bowl-shaped meadow came into view, and Slocum could see the Sioux ponies. Most of them were pintos and had brown and white patches indiscriminately splotched over their lean, muscled frames. They were smaller than the white man's horses, but were faster and had superior stamina when compared to the larger breeds favored by the white man.

Slocum dropped to one knee and peered out into the meadow. Because of the darkness, a dozen men could be hiding in the grass between him and the pony herd. He would have to step on one of them before he knew somebody was there, but it was unlikely that anyone would be watching the ponies. Anyway, he had no choice but to risk his plan.

He saw taller, darker shadows among the ponies and realized that the troopers might have turned some of their own horses out to graze with the herd. They could also be horses the Sioux had captured or taken in trade. But it might mean his own roan was somewhere out there, and he resolved to have a look, just in case.

Gray Fawn took the lead, circling back toward the base of the hill. She moved swiftly, but made no sound, and Slocum was hard-pressed to keep up with her. The horses seemed slightly on edge. Nickers rippled through the herd, and now and then one would run a few paces, as if something had startled it. Gray Fawn noticed the disquiet, and pulled Slocum down into the grass.

"Something is wrong," she said. "They are not usually like this. It is almost as if—"

She stopped and suddenly jabbed a finger toward a small group of ponies that had broken off from the herd. They ran twenty yards, then slowed to mill around but kept well apart from the others. Slocum watched closely, trying to pick up some movement, or a sound that didn't belong. Gray Fawn was right, the ponies were spooked, and there had to be some explanation.

Leaning close to her, he whispered, "Let's go ahead. Maybe we can find out what's got them so skittish." She didn't want to. He could tell by the way she nodded. It was more than reluctance, it was as if she felt obliged to do something she absolutely didn't want to do.

"Maybe it would be better if you waited here," he whispered.

She shook her head vigorously. "No, I'll go with you."

They crept along now, staying on their hands and knees as they approached the near edge of the herd. The horses were between them and the village, and it would be difficult for anyone near the lodges to see either of them as long as they stayed down. Slocum kept scanning the herd looking for his roan, but so far he hadn't caught a glimpse of him. It was so dark that many of the horses were little more than blotches of shadow. The fire in the village had died down, and only an occasional puff of wind kicked up sparks, so there was little light.

They were almost on the other side of the herd now, and there was still no sign of the roan. Slocum was prepared to leave without the big stallion, but he would have been much more comfortable with a familiar horse under him.

He stopped a moment, getting into a crouch and moving nearer to the herd. One of the nearby ponies whinnied and danced a step or two in his direction, then pawed the ground with one hoof. He heard a cry then, a little muffled blurt of surprise, and he looked for Gray Fawn, but couldn't see her. He couldn't risk calling out, even in a whisper, and dropped once more to his knees and crawled rapidly toward the direction of the sound. He pulled the Colt from his belt and held it in his right hand with his finger curled through the trigger guard.

Slowly, Gray Fawn materialized out of the darkness. She was on her knees, and beyond her was an indistinct shape. Slocum heard a whisper then, and realized that Gray Fawn was in conversation with someone.

He covered the last few yards and found her on her hands and knees leaning forward. And old man lay on the ground. He was whispering to her, and Slocum crawled alongside. Gray Fawn kept nodding.

"What is it?" Slocum whispered. "What's happening?"

But she hushed him with a sharp glance. Turning back to the old man, she bent low again. She would whisper a question and the old man would answer. Then, as casually as if he were used to crawling in the dark after midnight, the old man crept away toward the hill, leaving Gray Fawn and Slocum to stare after him.

"What is it?" Slocum asked again.

"Fights with Fire says many of the people have escaped from the village. There are about thirty still there, mostly women with children who could not be trusted to be silent."

"Where are they going?"

"They will go to the next village. Some of them have bows and arrows but most of them have no weapons. He says the soldiers are all drunk except for three guards, and they are frightened, so they stay together near the fire."

"Stay here," he said.

"Where are you going?" she asked, but he had already gotten to his feet and was sprinting in a crouch past the edge of the herd. He moved cautiously to some brush at the edge of the meadow, slowly working his way closer and closer to the village.

Near a stand of trees, just past the edge of the herd nearest the village, he caught sight of several of the troopers' horses. They were strung on a picket rope tied to a pair of cottonwoods. The horses had enough lead to allow them to graze on the thick blanket of grass that edged away from the cottonwoods and out into the meadow where the Sioux ponies roamed freely. One of them was his roan.

It was nearly one hundred yards to the nearest picketed horse, but he had to risk it. He wanted the roan, and he also wanted to cut the troopers' horses loose. If he was lucky, he might even succeed in driving off the Sioux ponies, but first he had to get to them.

Ducking low, he ran into the open keeping one eye on the village. There was no movement that he could see, and the village was absolutely silent. It would help if he knew where the sentries were, but he couldn't see the campfire from his position, and he was sure they would be somewhere close to it.

As he closed the gap to the picket rope he realized the roan was still saddled, as if he had been added to the picket as an afterthought. It was a break, one he hadn't expected, and one he didn't expect to be repeated. The troopers' horses fidgeted nervously as he bore down on them. One reared up and battered its hooves soundlessly against the shadows under the trees.

He slipped along the picket rope keeping the horses between him and the silent village, until he reached the tether for the roan. It was knotted tightly, and he clawed at it frantically. Glancing at the village through a gap between the roan and a big bay, he spotted something moving toward him. It was a figure stooped low and sprinting in fits and starts, pausing frozen for long seconds before darting another few yards and stopping again.

He couldn't see the figure clearly, but it seemed unlikely that it was one of the troopers. He dropped to one knee, pulled the stolen Colt and tucked it in the crook of his left elbow where he could get it quickly if he needed it as he worked on the knot.

There was movement behind him then, and he whirled, pistol in hand, to see Gray Fawn five feet away. Glancing back at the crouched figure, he reached out to pull the woman to the ground, covering his lips with one upright finger. Her lips parted as if to ask him what was going on, but he shook his head and she stayed quiet.

The figure was twenty yards away now. Slocum didn't believe that he'd been seen, and he stayed on one knee with the pistol in his hand while he waited to see what would happen. The figure darted the last twenty yards in a single burst, slipped in between the horses and crawled under the picket rope. Slocum was on the shadow in a flash, hooking an arm under its throat and covering its mouth with his other hand.

It was an old man, and Slocum whispered to Gray Fawn while his captive struggled to free himself. "Tell him it's all right. Tell him not to make any noise."

Gray Fawn crawled over to the struggling men, leaned forward and whispered in the old man's ear. Slocum felt him go limp, and he cautiously pulled his hand away from the old man's mouth. Still keeping his arm hooked around the old warrior's neck, Slocum relaxed the pressure enough for the man to answer Gray Fawn.

His name is Black Eagle, he says he wanted to stampede the horses," she explained.

Slocum said, "Tell him I was planning to do the same thing. Tell him that with his help, we should be able to do it."

Gray Fawn translated the message, still keeping her lips close to the old man's ear. The man moved suddenly, and waved a steel blade in front of Slocum's eyes. Its metal appeared dull gray in the darkness. Slocum let go, and Black Eagle moved along the picket rope, cutting each tether several feet away from the rope, making sure that not much lead was left to dangle from the horses' halters for anyone to grab hold of.

Slocum stepped closer to the roan, groped for the scabbard and found that his Winchester was still there. Moving to the saddlebags, he opened them, thinking he should get more ammunition for the carbine. Inside, he found his gunbelt coiled neatly, and his Colt Navy still in its holster. Strapping on the gunbelt, he moved back toward the picket rope with the roan's reins looped in one fist.

He handed the captured pistol to Gray Fawn, then reached back to give the Winchester to the old Sioux. The roan was the only saddled mount, but the Sioux were used to riding bareback. Their warriors preferred bareback riding or a simple, makeshift pad saddle to the heavier and more cumbersome Western or Mexican saddles the whites employed.

He pulled the two Indians into the shadows under the cottonwoods. Looking at the old man, he spoke to Gray Fawn. "Tell him we're only going to get one chance at this. Tell him we should make as little noise as possible. Try to drive the horses without using the guns. If we have to fire a few shots to run them off, let's do it together. Once they come out of the camp, the troopers will be disoriented. They won't be able to see well, but some of them will probably be sober enough to try to stop us."

Gray Fawn kept her eyes locked on Slocum's face as she translated phrase by phrase. The old man kept nodding his head and when Gray Fawn finished, he grunted that he understood.

"We should try to drive the ponies up over the hill behind the village. The soldiers won't dare to look for them in the dark, and that will give us a few hours head start. Understood?"

Once more, Gray Fawn translated, and once more the old man nodded and grunted. Then he reached out to clap Slocum on the shoulder. He whispered something in Lakota, and Gray Fawn translated.

"He says, 'Thank you.' "

"Too soon for that," Slocum whispered. "We haven't done it yet. Let's go."

He swung up into the saddle.

16

Slocum took the middle, Black Eagle rode on his right, bringing him closest to the village, and Gray Fawn was on Slocum's left, out of harm's way. The troopers' horses moved reluctantly at first, but Slocum lashed at them with a length of the picket rope and got them moving toward the pony herd. By the time they covered the one hundred yards to the main herd, they were moving at a fast trot. The horses tried to turn, but Gray Fawn and Black Eagle cut them off, forcing them to move straight ahead and on into the herd.

Time was working against them, and Slocum realized they'd have to work fast. He forced the roan ahead, and it shouldered its way through the tight knot of cavalry mounts. He raised his gun overhead, then whistled to get the attention of his allies. When both were ready, Slocum nodded and pulled the trigger. Almost instantaneously, shots were fired on either side of him, and the horses started to run.

He fired once more, and once again two more shots followed quickly on its heels. The Sioux ponies were running full tilt, and the bigger American horses were starting to gain on them. When they caught up, the mixed in and shouldered their way through the smaller, more agile Sioux ponies. The leading edge of the herd reached the long, gentle rise approaching the hill, then started to climb more sharply as it reached the base of the hill itself.

Behind him, Slocum could hear shouting, but he wouldn't look back to see what was happening. This was their one chance for escape, and he was determined to pull it off.

The roan reached the bottom of the hill and started up. Some ponies milled around in his wake but the majority of the Sioux mounts were charging up the hill. The ascent would slow them a little, and they might even decide to stop altogether, so Slocum fired once more. This time, he fired alone. He glanced toward Black Eagle, who was moving his horse toward the right wing of the herd to cut off several ponies that had veered off. The old man turned them back toward the main herd and fired the Winchester, letting it twirl in his hand to chamber another round, then fired another shot.

Gray Fawn was having problems of her own. A dozen pintos had spurted clear of the herd and were running parallel to the bottom of the hill. Gray Fawn was in pursuit, and Slocum called to her to come back, but she ignored him.

Gunshots started to crack behind them now, and Slocum glanced over his shoulder toward the village. He saw a handful of shadows running through the grass with bright muzzle flashes spearing from each. Bullets whistled past him, and two ponies on the slope ahead went down. The herd parted to race around them, and another pony stumbled as one of the downed animals tumbled into its path.

Slocum fired another shot, then lashed the roan to chase after Gray Fawn. She had reached the far side of the hill, and the terrified ponies were turning, but they were turning the wrong way and were heading back toward the village. Slocum angled away from the hill, racing to intercept them.

He wanted a clean sweep of all the ponies, if possible.

Cutting in front of the runaways, he blocked their path with the roan and fired as they galloped down on him full tilt. The gunshot turned them, and they veered to their left, now running back across the bottom of the hill. Slocum fired again, maneuvering to keep the roan between the hill and the village.

More gunshots exploded in the darkness, and one of the runaway ponies was hit in the shoulder. It lost its stride, fell, then whinnied as it tried to get to its feet. Slocum could see it had broken a foreleg, and shot it in the head as he galloped past.

The others veered again, heading away from the gunfire and racing for the hill. Slocum turned to follow them. Looking up, he could see Gray Fawn on the hilltop, waving for him to hurry. Another shot cracked behind him, this time from a rifle, and the bullet sailed past him so closely that he thought he could feel its heat. Charging up the hill, he spotted Black Eagle off to the right, still mounted, taking aim with the Winchester. The carbine barked, and Slocum heard a groan of pain from the meadow behind him.

A flurry of gunfire kicked up clots of dirt around the hooves of Black Eagle's mount, but he held it steady, aimed again, and fired. Slocum was nearly at the hilltop now, and Gray Fawn had backed away to get out of the line of fire from the meadow below. Black Eagle fired again, then wheeled his pony and vanished over the hilltop just as Slocum broke on top.

Charging down the far side, Slocum could see the ponies were still running, but had now broken into several smaller groups. When he hit the flats, Gray Fawn and Black Eagle had resumed their positions on either wing. There was a line of trees dead ahead, and they pushed the ponies on through it, and into the open plains beyond.

The ponies settled into a steady trot, while Slocum and the two Sioux concentrated on keeping the herd together. For the next hour, they let the herd set its own pace. They had managed to drive off most, possibly all of the cavalry mounts and nearly all of the Sioux ponies. Pursuit was, at best, a remote possibility.

When they had gone three or four miles, they were able to relax a little, and Slocum called a halt. Dismounting, Slocum patted the big roan on the flanks, then called to Gray Fawn and Black Eagle to join him.

"There isn't much time," Slocum said. "We can't keep herding the ponies because they slow us down too much. We have to get help, and the sooner we do, the better."

Black Eagle waited for Gray Fawn's translation, then held up a hand before Slocum could continue. He spoke rapidly, and Gray Fawn had to wait for him to finish before translating.

"Black Eagle says he can take the horses. He says I have to go with you because of the language, and because the Sioux in Two Elk's village are hostile to the white man. They would kill you before you got a chance to explain who you are and what you wanted."

"Makes sense," Slocum agreed, "but there's no way he can herd the ponies by himself."

"He says he can. He says as long as we get them moving, they will stay together, and he can keep them moving. It is only when they stop that it will be a problem, and he says that the further away from his village the horses are, the less likely it is that they'll be found."

Slocum was reluctant, but knew he had no choice. "Tell him all right, but tell him to be careful. Tell him that if bluecoats come, he should leave the horses and look out for himself."

Gray Fawn did as she was told and when she was finished, Black Eagle handed the Winchester to Slocum. He held out his hand, and Gray Fawn said, "I'll give him the pistol and the extra ammunition." She handed him the gun.

The old man nodded, tucked the pistol into his belt, and dropped the ammo pouch into his shirt. Handing the rifle to Gray Fawn, Slocum said, "You carry this."

Slocum climbed back onto the roan. It only took a few minutes to get the ponies moving again. Once they settled into their rhythm, Gray Fawn called for Slocum to follow her, and she veered off to the right. Slocum caught up to her and fell in beside her. "Where are we headed?" he asked.

"Two Elk's village is that way," she pointed toward the northeast, "about ten miles as the white man measures distance."

The sky was beginning to brighten, and Slocum was all too painfully aware of the clock ticking. He knew that the rest of Crum's detachment would probably leave the railroad survey camp soon after sunrise the following morning. It would take them most of the day to reach Black Eagle's village, but it was important to prevent them from joining up with Crum's unit, if at all possible. At best, they had thirty-six hours, and maybe a good deal less.

Gray Fawn rode easily. If anything, she was more at home on a horse than Slocum was himself, and her pony was more than equal to the pace she was setting. As the sky brightened, Slocum was able to scan the terrain ahead. Hill after hill after hill rolled away from them covered with lush grass that appeared pale gray in the predawn light.

He knew what he was about to do would be seen as treasonous by some, and that there were many white men who would be more than willing to drop a noose around his neck. But he couldn't worry about such things at the moment. If anyone was unable to see that he was taking the only reasonable course of action, then they would have to live with their ignorance. If he failed, they would have to suffer for it.

The sun came up when they had been riding a little over an hour. It was deep red, almost the color of blood for a few moments, then it brightened and turned orange as it climbed higher in the sky. Small, wispy clouds drifted across the horizon, as if floating just above the mountains to the east. They caught fire, burning from the edges inward, like balls of paper. Their centers were dark, and their perimeters glowed a brilliant orange that turned to yellow as the sun climbed all the way above the horizon.

Beautiful as it was, there was no time to stop and appreciate the magnificence of the sunrise. Human lives were hanging in the balance, red and white alike, and Slocum was determined to save as many of them as he could, no matter what the personal cost.

Staring at the sun through shaded eyes, he remembered that the second half of Lieutenant Crum's unit would be on the trail in twenty-four hours. That realization seemed somehow to communicate itself to the roan. He pulled even with Gray Fawn shouting for her to hurry, and to push her pony even harder. The urgency in his voice caused her to dig her heels into the pinto's flanks, and the smaller horse spurted ahead a few yards. Slocum used the reins to lash the roan into a faster gallop.

"How far now?" Slocum shouted

She looked back him, her braids flying, almost horizontal in the breeze "Not far," she answered. "Two miles, maybe three."

The horses were tired, and the toll was beginning to show on the gallant roan. But there was no time for pity, even for so valuable an ally as the great stallion beneath him. He would ride him until he was played out if he had to, and then he would run on foot, until he could no longer move his legs. Then he would crawl. He would keep moving until he reached the Sioux camp because it was his one and only chance to avert a bloody war.

Slocum was exhausted, and there were moments when he felt like he was wasting his time; that he should climb down from the saddle, curl up under a tree and go to sleep. He knew that if he did, when he woke up there would be blood in the grass in every direction. So he forced his eyes to stay open, and his hands to grip the reins.

Gray Fawn, was also near the breaking point. Each time she turned to look at him, he could see the dark circles under her eyes, the sag of her cheeks, and her sturdy shoulders seeming about to collapse. He worried that she might fall from her pony, but like him, she was determined.

Slocum realized that she had more at stake than he did. In any war, it was her people who would suffer the most. Their way of life was all but gone, and despite a determination to hang onto it as long as possible, it could not survive much longer, no matter what happened. There was no way the Sioux could win a war with the whites. Whether they realized it or not, they were too few, and too poorly armed. But they did deserve a chance to try and make the change to the white man's ways.

They broke over yet another ridge, and far below, Slocum saw a band of forest running the length of the valley. He knew there must be water somewhere among the trees and pointed. "We need to let the horses drink," he said.

"There is no time for that," Gray Fawn shouted back. "We have to keep going."

She veered toward the trees, but curved her path to run parallel to them, no more than fifty or sixty yards from the edge of the tree line.

Slocum was losing ground now; the roan was fighting its own exhaustion and slowly falling back. By the time they'd gone half the length of the valley, the woman was thirty yards ahead of him and starting to pull away even more rapidly. He called for her to slow up, but she was too far ahead to hear him over the pounding hooves.

When she was sixty yards ahead, he lashed the roan once more, but the great horse had nothing more to give. He was about to slow to a walk when there was a flurry of movement off to the left. Slocum barely caught sight of it out of the corner of his eye. When he turned, he saw a dozen Sioux charging toward him on horseback. They were painted for war.

He called once more to Gray Fawn, but she still didn't hear, and he pulled his Colt Navy and fired into the air. He saw her turn to see what had happened, then he pointed toward the advancing war party. There was no chance that he could outrun the Sioux ponies. The roan was nearly spent, and the Sioux mounts were probably fresh. He didn't want to use the gun to hold them off, but didn't know what else to do.

Gray Fawn turned her pony, wheeling in a great circle as the Sioux charged toward him, their war cries tearing the early morning silence to tatters.

Slocum slowed down, then reined in altogether. Holding his hands over his head, he slipped from the saddle.

The war party seemed to pick up speed. Slocum could see the bands of paint smeared across the chests and shoulders of the warriors, and the imprints of hands in red and black on the chests of the ponies. He looked once more for Gray Fawn. She was nearly four hundred yards away now, but closing in fast. The war party was half that distance, and the first hail of arrows flew toward him.

Several of the arrows sailed over his head and two slammed into the ground scant inches away. To spare the roan, Slocum moved away from the exhausted horse and braced himself for the onslaught. One of the warriors, a big man with a lightning bolt slashing across his chest, was pulling out ahead of the others—maybe because he had the best pony or maybe he was the most eager for counting coup. Slocum didn't know, and didn't care.

The warrior had a lance that he lowered when he was twenty-five yards away. Slocum crouched, but held his ground. The point of the lance glittered in the red sunlight as if it had already been dipped in blood. At fifteen yards, Slocum could see the warrior curl his lips back into a smile. When he was ten yards away, Slocum made his move, feinting to the right, then cutting left, denying the warrior time to change the position of his lance.

As the horse closed in on him, Slocum used the last of his strength to hurl himself at the warrior. He caught him in the chest with his right shoulder, and sent him tumbling from the charging pony. The impact knocked the wind from both men, but the warrior was the first to recover. He got to his knees as the rest of the Sioux encircled both men, their war cries were horrendous and deafening. Slocum felt a hand slap his back, and then a bow prod him in the ribs, but no one was going to deprive the man with the lightning bolt the chance to kill this white man. So the rest of the Sioux stayed on their mounts, urging their companion forward.

The warrior charged and Slocum kicked him in the stomach. With the last of his strength he fell on his adversary, closing his hands around the warrior's throat. He saw a knife on the Sioux's hip and grabbed for it, missed, then closed one hand over the warrior's wrist as he reached for the blade.

A gunshot froze both men. Another one parted the circle of shrieking warriors, who then fell silent as if they had been struck dumb.

Gray Fawn rode into the circle and dismounted.

17

Slocum breathed a sigh of relief. The man beneath him continued to struggle for several seconds until Gray Fawn walked over to Slocum and yanked him away. "Leave him alone," she shouted. "Stop it, all of you. Stop it!"

The Sioux started whispering among themselves as Gray Fawn hauled Slocum to his feet. The warrior on the ground glared up at him as if he was angry that he had been saved by a mere woman. Slocum steeled himself for a renewed attack, but the warrior got to his feet slowly, and brushed himself off. Then he said something to Gray Fawn.

She answered, then turned to Slocum. "My brother wants to know why I interfered. He says he was ready to kill you."

"And what did you tell him?" Slocum asked.

She smiled then. "I told him it seemed to be the other way around. He didn't like it."

"I don't blame him. You've made him look like a fool."

"You made yourselves look like fools, both of you. Men!" She turned away and said something to her brother, then placed her hands on his chest and shoved him. He shook his head as if he was completely baffled. His gesture showed that understanding women was something he had struggled with all his life, failed miserably to accomplish, and now despaired of ever achieving.

He glared at Slocum once more over his sister's shoulder, then turned and grabbed his horse by the war rope which another warrior was holding out to him. Swinging up onto the back of the pony, he rode off, leaving the rest of the warriors to stare after him.

"Where is he going?" Slocum asked.

"Home, where he should have been all along," Gray Fawn said. "I told him why we have come, but just a little. It is better if I explain everything to my father."

"Your father? I thought we were going to a village under Two Elks."

"We are. Two Elks is my father."

"Why in hell didn't you tell me that?"

"It changes nothing. Now, get on your horse." She pushed him the same way she pushed her brother, and the warriors laughed. He was certain his face wore the same look of bafflement her brother's face had worn.

He walked over to the roan who was idly munching grass and paying no attention whatsoever to the goings on. Slocum swung into the saddle and waited for Gray Fawn to mount her pony, then fell in alongside her.

"Who are these men?" he asked. "Are they all your relatives?"

She laughed. "No, they are members of the Crow Owners, an *akicita*." They are like your police. They are in charge of keeping the people secure when the village moves from one place to another. They try to keep peace in the village, too. They are among the best warriors. It is a great honor to be asked to join an *akicita*."

"Like the Dog Soldiers of the Cheyenne?"

She nodded. "Like them, yes. Not exactly, but like them." Her voice couldn't disguise the conviction that he would never understand the difference, and that it was pointless to try to explain.

"Will your father—?"

She cut him off. "We should wait until we get to the village. I want to rest. You should rest, too. There is so much to do and so little time. After we eat and bathe, we can sleep a while then we will meet with the council and tell them what has happened. They don't know that more soldiers are coming."

"Can you control them?"

She shook her head. "No. Women are not part of the council. I will tell my father and he will have to argue with the other members. So will you."

"But—"

"They will hear you. I will see to it."

"But—"

"I don't want to talk now," she said. "I want to think. Please be quiet."

Slocum lapsed into silence. He was conscious of so many images flooding in around him. He was riding in the middle of a full-blown Sioux war party, following a woman he'd know for less than forty-eight hours into a Sioux village, in the heart of hostile Indian country. At the same time, he knew that soldiers would soon be on their way to punish Indians who had done nothing more than defend themselves by punishing white men who had committed cold-blooded murder. His head was spinning at the prospect of having to stand up in front of a council of war chiefs and make his case for patience. The prospects for success were not good, and he knew it.

The warriors crowded in around him, riding as close as they dared and staring at him. Their looks were open and curious, rather than hostile. It must seem to them, he thought, that he had quite a story to tell. Slocum didn't disagree.

The sun was well up in the sky now, and the territory ahead was flooded with brilliant light. When the village came into view, its lodges were so starkly lit by the sun, that their contours seemed almost bleached away, and the entire scene looked like it had been cut out of paper. It reminded him of photographs he had seen, the only difference being the pale colors instead of the flat black and white.

People spilled out of the lodges to join others already arrayed at the edge of the village. Presumably, they had been alerted by Gray Fawn's brother when he reached the village. There were some hostile faces, but most of the Sioux seemed reserved, as if they were prepared to wait and see what might happen. The strange white man who had just ridden into their midst was something of a novelty.

Gray Fawn dismounted, and Slocum followed her example. A young boy, no more than ten, took the reins from his hands and patted the roan on the neck, then ran his fingers over the sweat-darkened hide. The animal bobbed its head and nuzzled the boy's palm, which held a handful of grain.

Gray Fawn gestured for him to follow her, then ducked into the entrance of the nearest lodge. Inside, it was dark and smelled of the same sweet honeysuckle as Gray Fawn herself. A small fire burned in the fire pit, casting wan orange light on the walls, where shadows rose and fell in time to the flickering of the flames.

An older man, with a face like fine leather and thick hands that rested calmly in his lap, looked up as Slocum entered, but betrayed no emotion. Skirting the fire pit, Gray Fawn walked over to the man then leaned down and kissed him on the forehead. She whispered something in Lakota, and while the man studied his white visitor, his head canted toward the woman.

When she finished speaking, Gray Fawn straightened up and the man nodded before looking at Slocum more intently. "Why do you care what happens to my people?" he asked.

Surprised by the English, Slocum thought that this man, who was almost certainly Two Elks, was not prone to beating about the bush. Before he could answer, the man said, "My daughter tells me that you risked your life to save hers. For that I thank you. That is not something the Lakota see often."

Slocum shrugged. "It was nothing, I . . ." He stopped, not knowing what to say and afraid that anything he did say might be misconstrued.

"Gray Fawn, your friend is a man of few words," the man said.

Feeling the least bit foolish, Slocum circled the fire pit and stuck out a hand. "John Slocum," he said. "Pleased to meet you."

The man nodded, taking the hand in his own firm grip. "Two Elks is my name in English," he said. "Thank you for helping my daughter."

"It was the right thing to do," he said.

"Many times men know the right thing to do and still they do not do it. It takes courage to follow the right road. I wish there were more men like that in this world. But. . . ." It was the chief's turn to shrug, there were some things that couldn't be expressed in words. His profound sadness at the inadequacy of mankind seemed to squeeze the chief a bit until he regained control of himself.

"You must be tired and hungry. We will talk later, after you have had a chance to wash and rest. Gray Fawn will help you."

He gave Slocum a look, but if there was something specific on his mind, the chief thought better of saying so.

Gray Fawn took him by the hand and pulled him toward the entrance to the lodge. Outside, people were still milling about, and crowded in around the pale-skinned visitor as he emerged. Some of the children reached out to touch him as he moved past, and tagged along behind Gray Fawn like puppies on leashes.

"Where are we going?" Slocum asked, as they reached the edge of the village. She turned, but instead of answering his question, she shouted at the people crowding Slocum on all sides, they fell back, their faces looking embarrassed. One or two of the women shouted back at her, and she glared fiercely.

"What did they say?" Slocum asked.

"Nothing that concerns you," she said.

She pulled his hand again, dragging him out into the grass. They walked toward a herd of ponies grazing contentedly nearby, skirted the edge of the herd, and headed for a dense willow grove across the meadow. The lush branches swept the ground as they undulated in the breeze.

When they reached the willows, Gray Fawn turned once more, as if to make certain they had not been followed and, satisfied, stepped through the leafy curtain into the shade.

Slocum could hear water ahead, and it dawned on him that Gray Fawn was leading him to a place where he could bathe. When they reached the edge of the creek he could see that more willows lined the opposite bank. All around them, the branches of the willows dipped toward the water. Sunlight filtered through the leaves and splashed on the water's surface. There was an opening at either end of the shaded grove, but it was protected from all but the most deliberate of prying eyes.

Gray Fawn said, "You might want to wash your clothes. I will bring other clothing for you. I'll come back in a little while."

Before he could say a word, she slipped back into the dense willow branches and disappeared. He heard the swish of the leaves against her as she passed back the way they had come in. With a shrug, he sat down on the mossy ledge at the water's edge, shucked off his clothes and slipped into the creek. Despite the shade, the water was warm, and it flooded over him as he pushed off from the bank and floated into deeper water toward the middle of the creek.

It felt good to lie there; his aching muscles relaxed for the first time in what seemed like weeks. The water's warmth seeped into him, and a great tiredness swept like a wave over him. He stared for a while up at the canopy of willow branches, then closed his eyes. Using his hands and flexing his joints, he worked the knots out of his body, and rubbed his skin trying to rid it of the accumulated sweat and grime.

He worried that he might actually fall asleep, and forced his eyes open. He watched the current swirl around him, as stray bits of straw, an occasional leaf, and even a single purple flower held afloat by its petals drifted past.

He barely heard the noise in the willows until Gray Fawn stepped onto the bank, her moccasins were soft and silent on the moss. In her arms, she held a bundle of buckskin—the promised change of clothes, he guessed. She set it beside his boots, and walked upstream to disappear through the branches once more without having said a word.

He heard a soft splash a few moments later and glanced toward the bright arch of sunlight upstream. Then he saw her paddling out into the middle and turning on her back to float, as he had done. The mounds of her breasts broke the surface, and one leg rose up as she turned on her stomach and stroked across the deepest part of the creek.

He turned on his stomach and buried his face in the water as he stroked his way against the current. He didn't look up until he felt her hand on his head pushing him deeper into the water. He shook her off and spluttered to the surface. She was laughing, standing in water up to her stomach.

He swam the few feet that separated them, and reached out and caught her by one hip. This time she made no attempt to fend him off. Instead, she sank to her knees, leaving just her face above the water. Suddenly, she ducked under the surface and darted past him like a trout. Her hand raked his thigh as she groped for, and found his erection.

Then, she let go, and swam around behind him. She stood again while pressing herself against him. He could feel the sharp prod of her erect nipples, and her damp bush as she ground her hips against him for a moment. Then she pulled away, and hit the water in a shallow dive as he turned to swim for the bank.

Slocum stumbled after her, catching her just as she pulled herself out onto the mossy ledge. He followed her out of the creek as she turned on her knees to face him. Hard as a rock, he nearly came in her hand as she curled her fingers around him. She pulled him toward her and opened her mouth to take him in. He felt the slickness of her tongue as it snaked around the head of his cock. The warmth of her was overwhelming and his knees felt as if they had turned to jelly. He closed his eyes, tilted his head back, and gasped as she pulled back, nipping him with her teeth as she let him slide away.

She was grinning when he looked at her again. She reached out and grabbed him once more, this time to pull him down. His knees sank into the moss between her legs as she lay back, spreading them wide and continuing to lead him.

He felt the slickness of her, and the thick flesh of her lips parting as he slid in. She closed in around him, and wrapped her arms around his waist pulling him closer and closer. Her hips were thrusting, and her arms compressing him as if she sought to merge their two bodies into one.

She moaned then, and brought her legs up past his hips to let him probe still deeper. Her muscles felt like the softest velvet as they rippled the full length of him, coaxing him to move deeper and faster. Her hips pumped against him and her breath came faster and faster as she urged him on.

Leaning forward, he placed his weight on his outstretched arms. He drove harder and harder, his own breath exploding with every thrust until she quivered and moaned once more, then let out a long, shuddering sigh. He felt himself explode deep inside her then, and lay his head on her breast and closed his eyes.

He was aware only of the stroke of her fingers down his spine and the soft hiss of her breathing—and for at least a little while, that was all he cared about.

18

Slocum woke up to find Gray Fawn staring at him. Her hand was on his shoulder, rocking him gently. "It's time for the council," she said.

He groaned and sat up. The buckskin leggings felt strange to him, and for a moment he was disoriented. She smiled. "You don't look so much like a white man, now," she said.

"I don't feel much like a white man, to tell you the truth," he answered.

"Hurry. Two Elks is anxious to know what is happening, and there will be trouble from some of the younger warriors. Many of them want to make war, and it will be difficult to stop them."

Slocum nodded and got to his feet. She handed him a plain shirt, also made of buckskin. He slipped it over his head, then sat down again to pull on his boots. He followed her outside into bright sunlight. Instinctively, he reached for his pocket watch, but there was no pocket, and no watch, and that threw him for another loop.

Gray Fawn led the way to the council lodge. The sides

were rolled partway up to let in the breeze, and he could see seven or eight men sitting around a small fire. Two Elks was talking to Gray Fawn's brother, Long Bow, the young firebrand who had charged him with a lance the night before. The young warrior looked up and glared at Slocum as he entered.

Two Elks pointed to an empty place in the loose circle, gesturing for Slocum to sit down. He did as he was told, while the other warriors examined him as if he were some sort of biological specimen.

"Two Elks, I thank you for—"

But the chief held up a hand. "First we must smoke the council pipe," he said. It was already packed, and he used a thin straw to catch a flame from the small fire. He lit the pipe and raised it overhead, then pointed it toward each of the four compass directions before taking a puff. He passed it to his right, and each of the council members in turn took a puff and passed it on.

When it reached him, Slocum made as if to pass it on to the man on his right, but Two Elks stopped him. "You must smoke the pipe, too," he said. "All who would speak in the council must smoke."

"I didn't know whether or not it was acceptable for me to take part in a sacred ritual," Slocum said, taking the pipe back. He nodded to the chief, and took a puff of the strong tobacco. Fighting the urge to cough, he handed the long, ornately carved pipe to the next warrior.

When the last man had smoked, the pipe was passed back to Two Elks. He puffed once more, and again elevated the pipe, then tapped it on a rock at the edge of the fire pit to dislodge the ashes. "Tell us what you know about the bluecoats," Two Elks said.

Before Slocum could respond, Tall Shadow stood up. In Lakota, he asked, angrily, "Why are you using the white

man's language? This is a Sioux council. You should use
our language."

Two Elks raised a hand to calm his son and said in
English, "We have a guest, and the guest does not know
our language. It is not right to make it difficult for him when
he is trying to help."

Once more in Lakota, Tall Shadow argued his point.
"Most of the members of the council do not speak the
white man's tongue, and—"

But Two Elks snapped at him again in English. "Sit
down. You will have your turn to speak. Now it is the
time for John Slocum to tell us what he knows." Then, as
if to reassure both his son and Slocum, he added, "And I
will interpret for us."

Then, he nodded to Slocum, and folded his hands in
his lap. Slocum was impressed by the chief's dignity. He
understood why Tall Shadow was angry, and knew that he
would feel the same way if circumstances were reversed,
but Two Elks was right. There was no time to waste on
petty arguments.

Quickly, he outlined what had happened at Black Eagle's
Village. He explained how Crum's men had captured the
village, and that the women and children were being held
hostage. He told them Crum had sent two messengers to
ask the rest of his unit to join him the following day, and
that Fort McAllister was being notified of the situation.

"Will the soldier fort send more bluecoats to Black Eagle's
village?" Two Elks asked.

Slocum shook his head with uncertainty. "I don't know.
I know that Colonel Roberts at Fort McAllister has always
been a friend to the Sioux. I don't think he would do anything hasty, but it will depend on what Crum tells him."

"And why do you care what happens to us?" Two Elks
asked.

Slocum considered the question. He knew it had been asked not out of skepticism, but simply for information. But he also knew that some of the young warriors around the fire were very skeptical indeed, and that they must assume that he had some ulterior motive. He didn't blame them, and doubted that anything he said would convince them their suspicions were unfounded—but he had to try.

"This is beautiful country," he began, and when Two Elks translated, even the firebrands gave the "Hou!" of assent. "And I know that there are many white men who wish to take the land away from you. But there are also many men who think as I do, that what belongs to the Sioux is theirs to keep. Such men think it is wrong to cause trouble to make an excuse for war so that the land can be taken from the Sioux."

"But you work for the railroad, and we never said the railroad could come here," Two Elks pointed out. "The treaty we signed in 1868, where Red Cloud and Spotted Tail touched the pen to the peace paper, said that as long as there were buffalo here, the land was ours, and that no white man could come without asking for permission. No one has ever asked for that permission, and it has never been given, yet the white men come in their wagons and they build roads through our land, and they make their railroad."

"I understand, and I think that is wrong."

"Then why do you work for the railroad?"

"Because I was told that permission had been given. Then I learned that it had not, but I was told that a treaty was being negotiated now with Red Cloud that would give permission. Because the railroad can only be built in good weather, it was decided to go ahead. That was risky, but . . ." he shrugged. He really didn't have an excuse, and he knew it. He couldn't lie, and didn't even want to, so he said nothing.

"How do you think we can stop the war before it starts?" Two Elks asked.

Here, Slocum was on surer ground. "I know that the killing of the white men near where Red Bear was murdered will be an excuse some white men will use to make war. But I also know that one of the white men who was killed had murdered Red Bear. I think that if Gray Fawn can explain this to Colonel Roberts, this will prevent the war from starting."

Tall Shadow raised a hand to be heard, and Two Elks nodded. In English, the young warrior said, "The bluecoats will say that the Sioux who killed those white men are criminals. They will say that they must be punished. They will say that unless they are given to the bluecoats so they can be hanged, then all Sioux will be considered criminals. That is always the way it is. Always when a white man kills a Sioux, the bluecoats look the other way. And always when the Sioux protect themselves, when they take for themselves the justice that the white man talks about but never offers, then the Sioux are said to be bad men. This time will be no different."

Two Elks looked to Slocum to defend his argument. "What Tall Shadow says is the truth," Two Elks said. "Why should the colonel at the fort listen to Gray Fawn? In the past, when a Sioux tried to tell his story, he was thrown in the white man's jail. Sometimes even hanged, even though he had done nothing wrong. Why will it be different now?"

"Because Colonel Roberts is a fair man, and because I will also speak for the Sioux. They will not hang me for telling the truth."

"Do not be so sure," Tall Shadow snapped.

"But I *am* sure."

"What do you think we should do?" another young warrior named Runs Too Slow asked.

"The village of Black Eagle is under the control of Lieutenant Crum. He has eight men with him. There would be danger to the hostages if the village were to be attacked. I think we have to find some way to bargain with Crum. If we can offer him something in exchange for leaving the village, then we can go a long way toward ending the troubles," Slocum answered.

"What would you offer him?" Tall Shadow demanded. "Should we give up the Powder River country? Should we say go on and build your railroad? Is that what you want us to do?"

"No," Slocum said. "I have a better idea."

"I don't want to hear your ideas. I don't trust you. You are white just as this lieutenant of the bluecoats is."

"Let him speak!" Two Elks shouted. "Listen to what he has to say before you refuse. He is trying to help. Would you prefer to attack Black Eagle's village? Do you want the blood of women and children on your hands, all because you are too hotheaded to listen to a man whose skin is not like yours?"

Once more, the council members said, "Hou!" Tall Shadow glared at them, but he knew better than to push his luck, and he sat down.

"I will listen," he said.

"Good," Two Elks replied. His voice made it clear that Tall Shadow had better be as good as his word, or he would have to answer to his father.

"If we can capture the second unit of bluecoats," Slocum suggested, "then we will have something to offer Crum."

"But as soon as he frees the people in the village, you will have to let the bluecoats go. What will stop him from turning around and attacking the village all over again, this time with twice as many bluecoats?" Two Elks said.

"Who said we would let them go?" Slocum said.

"You cannot lie to him," Two Elks said. "You cannot kill them. What would you do?"

"You'll see. It will work, I am certain, but first we have to capture the bluecoats coming from the survey camp. I know the route they will take, and we should try to find some place along that route where we can capture them without running the risk of having to fight them."

"That is not possible," Runs Too Slow said. "This is just foolishness. We cannot do it. Better to attack the village, where the number of bluecoats is small, and take our chances."

"No, we can do it," Tall Shadow said. "I know where, and I know how."

Two Elks nodded. "Are you sure?"

"Yes. You know the canyon with one end only?"

"A box canyon?" Slocum asked.

"Yes, a box canyon. That is what the white soldiers call it. If we can decoy the bluecoats inside, then we can capture them," Tall Shadow said.

"It's a long shot," Slocum said.

"But we don't have any other choice."

"Except war. . . ." Slocum said.

"Yes," Two Elks answered. "Except war. We will have to try it."

"I will need all the warriors we can gather," Tall Shadow said. "The bluecoats will have to know that they do not have a chance of shooting their way out. That is the only way to avoid shooting altogether. If they think they can beat us, they will try."

"We can't let that happen," Slocum said. "Tell me why you changed your mind?"

"Because," Tall Shadow said, "I have to care about my people. I cannot stand back and let a white man do more to save them than I am willing to do. That would be shameful. I would not be worthy of being a chief, and someday I will be."

Two Elks looked around the council. "Does anyone have anything to say?" he asked, the Lakota language sounding sharp and guttural. No one moved. No one raised a hand. No one said a word.

"Good, then we will do as Tall Shadow suggests."

19

They left at dawn. Two Elks had assembled a formidable force. More than one hundred warriors, chosen not only for their courage in battle but also for their willingness to follow instructions and maintain discipline, rode off with Tall Shadow in the lead. Gray Fawn stayed well in the rear, surrounded by a knot of the best warriors for her protection. Slocum tried several times to catch a glimpse of her, but he had no luck.

Tall Shadow no longer seemed so distant, and Slocum thought that perhaps the young Sioux was beginning to trust him. At the same time, the warrior allowed more of his personality to show by demonstrating a keen wit and a mischievous sense of humor.

He explained to Slocum how he had grown up near Fort Laramie, where a number of bands of Miniconjou and Oglala Sioux had spent some of their summers. They weren't as tame as Laramie Loafers, but they were not as wild and remote as the Hunkpapas who tended to stay farther north, away from the Oregon Trail. All the Sioux had come to call the trail the Holy Road because they were forbidden to harass any white men passing through on their way to Oregon Territory.

On the ride, both men were able to relax a little, and Slocum found that Tall Shadow was willing to speak candidly. "How did you and Gray Fawn learn to speak English so well?" Slocum asked.

"I learned English from Caspar Collins, a bluecoat lieutenant who was interested in the Sioux. Each of us taught the other his language. My father was with Young Man Afraid of His Horses then. Crazy Horse was there. He knew Caspar Collins, too. They were friends."

"Where is Collins now?" Slocum asked.

"Dead."

"In the war?"

Tall Shadow shook his head. "No, at Upper Platte Bridge. He was the only white friend I ever had. It was painful to lose him, to watch him die."

"You were there?"

Tall Shadow nodded. "I was young then, not yet twenty winters, but I was there. He died like a brave man, trying to save one of his bluecoat soldiers who was wounded. Young Man Afraid of His Horses also knew him, and liked him very much. He ran out of the brush along the creek trying to tell him to go back. Caspar looked at him, but I don't know if he understood what Young Man Afraid of His Horses was trying to tell him. I think so, but. . . ."

The young warrior fell silent then. He cleared his throat, and Slocum understood that the death of his friend was still very much with him. Rather than try to change the subject, Slocum kept his own silence. A five hour ride brought them to the box canyon, and Tall Shadow rode into its center with Slocum alongside.

The canyon was deceptive. It had a sharp dogleg to the left, and from the outside it appeared to be a canyon like any other. Only when the dogleg was reached did the sheer stone wall at the far end loom up in front of a man. The rimrock up above was littered with huge boulders, many of which seemed to teeter on the very edge, as if a strong gust of wind would send them plummeting to the canyon floor below.

Clumps of thick brush were scattered across the floor, and became thicker along the small creek that cut through the sandy bottom. Bands of heavier brush lined the walls on either side, not at their bases, where steep mounds of scree from the walls above had collected, but further away from the foot of each wall. A kind of channel ran between the stone heaps and the brush, where falling rocks had made it difficult for anything to root and grow.

"I see what you mean," Slocum said. "It's perfect. *If*— and it's a big if—we can get them in here."

"We'll get them in here," Tall Shadow said. "I have been on decoy rides with Crazy Horse and Gall. I know how to do it, and so do my warriors."

Slocum nodded. "I don't want anything to go wrong, Tall Shadow. I don't want these men hurt. If anything happens to them, whatever chance we have of avoiding an all out war will be destroyed."

"I understand. I will see to it. The young men are angry, and they are restless, but they will do as my father has explained to them, and as I have explained to them."

"You're sure?"

Tall Shadow shrugged. "Are you sure *your* plan will work?"

"I guess I will stay on the canyon floor with your men. It will be important to make the bluecoats understand quickly that they will not be harmed."

Tall Shadow grunted. "My sister will stay here with you so you can talk to the warriors. Some of them speak a little English, but. . . ."

" . . . but they're not likely to," Slocum said, finishing the sentence Tall Shadow had left dangling.

"Yes, they are not likely to." He gestured to one of the warriors and waved him over. "This is Hunts With a Knife," he said, introducing the warrior to Slocum.

Slocum extended a hand, and the warrior took it reluctantly. Tall Shadow then spoke rapidly in Lakota. Hunts With a Knife listened intently, asked two quick questions, and then nodded to show he understood.

Turning to Slocum, Tall Shadow said, "I told him that you will arrange the warriors where you think it is best for them to be, and that my sister will act as interpreter for you. I told him that anything you say should be treated as if my father said it."

"Your father is a wise man, Tall Shadow. I don't know if you have insulted him or not." He smiled, and Tall Shadow laughed.

"If I have, I'm sure he will hear about it," he said. "My sister will be sure to tell him. She can never keep a secret."

He turned away and started toward his pony. Four warriors were already on their mounts, one of them holding Tall Shadow's pinto by the war rope. "Tall Shadow," Slocum called.

The Sioux stopped and turned. Slocum stepped closer to him. "Be careful," he said. "It is a dangerous thing you are doing. As long as the bluecoats think they have you outnumbered, they will not be afraid of you. They will follow you, but they will also shoot at you."

Tall Shadow grinned. "I learned how to do this from Crazy Horse. Nothing has hurt him, and nothing will hurt me, either."

With that, he leaped onto his pony, and gave a shout

as he dug in his heels and drove the pony into a quick gallop. His war cry echoed off the walls of the canyon and was quickly picked up by the rest of the Sioux. The terrifying howls and their hundreds of echoes peaked in a thunderous cacophony. Slocum held up a hand, and they stopped, the last cries echoing off one wall after another, their sound eroding with every reverberation until they were heard no more.

Suddenly, there was a silence so perfect that the canyon may have been devoid of life. Then, Slocum saw Gray Fawn for the first time since leaving the village. She walked toward him, her stride confident but her eyes shyly averted.

"We have to hurry," Slocum said. "We have to get these men into position."

"You sound like a bluecoat officer," she said.

He smiled. "Today, I am a Sioux officer, Gray Fawn—and proud of it."

"I want to thank you for what you are trying to do, John Slocum. My father thinks you are a brave man, the bravest white man he has ever seen, braver even than my brother's friend, Caspar Collins."

"Tall Shadow told me about him," he said. He didn't want to say more, and he knew he didn't have to.

Rubbing his chin, he said, "I think I better have a good look at this place. Come with me, and bring Hunts With a Knife." He walked deeper into the canyon and examined the walls. For a moment, he considered the possibility of keeping all of the men up top, but dismissed the idea when he realized that there was too much cover on the canyon floor. In order to keep Crum's second unit from the temptation of shooting their way out of the canyon, he knew he had to have the bulk of his men close. However, the rimrock would be useful. The soldiers would not know how many Sioux were up top, and the initial shock of seeing warriors all around them might freeze them enough to allow the Sioux to make a second, more dramatic move.

Pointing to the rim, he explained what he wanted. Hunts with a Knife chose his men carefully and sent them out of the canyon and up to the top. Continuing his survey, Slocum started picking spots that offered both concealment and protection. He knew there was a chance that once the troopers realized they were trapped, they would panic and start shooting wildly. If that happened, he wanted to make sure that no one got hurt. The Sioux were under strict instructions not to shoot unless Slocum gave the order.

When he had positioned all of the warriors remaining on the canyon floor, he walked back to the middle of the canyon and placed himself about two hundreds yards in from the dogleg. Taking cover behind a tangle of scrub oak and a cluster of huge boulders, he looked at the sky. He knew there was a possibility, how great he couldn't guess, that the decoy party might fail. They might miss the cavalry altogether, or they might fail to lure them into the canyon. There was even the chance, although it was slim, that in the first flurry of contact the troopers capture or kill the decoy party. He tried to push such bleak thoughts aside, but he knew he wasn't going to be able to relax until he saw Tall Shadow come back.

Gray Fawn wanted to stay with him, but he insisted that she stay well back in the canyon with a small band of warriors. If bullets started flying, he wanted her out of the way. It was her story, after all, on which everything hinged. If she were to die, any chance for peace would die with her.

He knelt behind the boulders, alternately looking at the rim, and craning his neck to check the placement of the warriors in the brush. It was a good layout, and he knew he had a chance if the decoy team managed to pull off its end of the strategy.

Once, he saw a warrior leaning out over the rimrock, and he got to his feet and shouted. The man waved to him, and Slocum gestured frantically for the man to duck back out of sight. The warrior waved back gaily, until Gray Fawn, from far back in the canyon, yelled at him in Lakota. Slocum heard the other warriors chuckling, and was dying to know what she had said, but there was no time to find out. Whatever she'd said, it had the desired effect. The warrior vanished.

Every little thing gnawed at him. A nickering horse drew his wrath. An overheard whisper drew him out from behind cover to stalk the whisperer and give him a tongue-lashing that he didn't understand, but would never forget.

Slocum's nerves were frayed, threatening to snap at any moment. He knew the Sioux were not used to discipline, and he was starting to understand how the waiting must be driving them crazy. It was driving *him* crazy, and it was his idea. For men used to doing whatever they wanted, whenever they wanted to, crouching behind these stones and baking under the scorching sun must have been worse than agony.

Without a watch, time weighed heavily on him. He kept looking at the sky, trying to estimate how much longer he'd have to wait, knowing that even as he looked up, there was no way for him to be sure. He heard the cry of a hawk, and thought someone was coming. A deer darted across the dogleg and plunged into the creek, and he swore it was a horseman.

And still no one came.

He was surrounded by more than one hundred hostile Indians, but he'd never felt more alone in his life. He kept fighting the urge to get up and go back to where Gray

Fawn was waiting, just to have someone to talk to. He'd seen combat in the war, and he had more than his share of waiting to numb the mind, but this was different. This time there was no one he could share a gripe with, no one to play cards with, or exchange a joke. There were no officers to mock, and worst of all, there was no enemy to hate.

Then he heard the gunshot. It came from far off, and it was so faint that he thought for a moment he might have imagined it. Then there was another, and then a third.

He heard yips then, coming closer. The decoy, he hoped. And prayed. More gunfire, sporadic, half hearted, cracked, a little closer now, and then he could hear the pounding of hooves. Closer and closer they came, so close that he could hear the beat of individual hooves on the dry ground echoing off the walls around the bend in the canyon.

The decoy party burst around the bend. Tall Shadow was bringing up the rear, and firing his pistol over his shoulder. Slocum felt every muscle in his body turn to stone. He thought for a moment he wasn't going to be able to move. The decoys thundered on by and, a moment later, their arrival signalled by another flurry of gunshots, a dozen men broke around the dogleg, their big horses lathered in sweat, their tongues lolling. They had been ridden hard, and the pace was taking its toll.

Slocum got to his feet, feeling the tension drain out of him with no warning. He felt suddenly relaxed. Keeping under cover, he moved around the largest boulder, his arm held high overhead. The troopers thundered past, and he recognized Warren Anderson and Barney Tormey with them.

He brought his hand down, and the rimrock exploded. Thirty warriors gave vent to their war cries, and the horrifying howls filled the canyon once more.

Slocum raised his pistol and fired two quick shots into

the air as the troopers skidded to a halt. One of then turned, and Slocum saw the terror on his face. The trooper realized that he had been duped—that they all had been—and his wild eyes darted this way and that as he looked for some way out of the trap.

A hail of arrows sailed down into the canyon, spearing the earth all around the terrified white men. Slocum slipped from behind the boulders and stepped out into the open.

"Warren," he shouted. "Warren, listen to me. You have nothing to be afraid of."

Anderson spun in his saddle. "Slocum, what the hell . . .?"

One of the troopers fired a shot, the bullet narrowly missing Slocum, and ricocheting off the boulder behind him before whining away and slamming into the canyon wall.

Slocum took another step forward, and then a third. "Warren, listen to me! Put down your guns. No one is going to hurt you."

He walked toward Anderson's horse, keeping his hands high so that the troopers could see him.

"Gone over to the other side, have you, Slocum?" Anderson snapped.

"No, not at all."

"Then what the hell do you call this?"

One of the troopers raised his rifle, but Barney reached out and grabbed it by the barrel. "Let the man have his say, lad," he said.

"Lieutenant Crum made a bad mistake, Warren," Slocum said.

"Dead is he? Is that what you're telling me?"

Slocum shook his head. "No. He's not dead, but if we don't do something fast, he will be, and the rest of us, too. I'll tell you what happened, but I want your guns on the ground, first. All of them."

One of the troopers sneered, "Suppose we don't do like you say?"

Slocum raised his hand again, then brought it down, and the rest of the Sioux swarmed out of the brush. "I think you'd better, trooper," he said.

20

They made a strange caravan; a dozen unarmed white men, ten wearing the blue coats of the United States Army, and two, Warren Anderson and Barney Tormey, looking slightly out of place in their civilian clothes. Strangely, they didn't look quite as nervous as their fellow cavalry captives. They were surrounded by more than one hundred fully armed Sioux warriors painted for war.

Slocum rode beside them with Tall Shadow and Hunts With a Knife keeping him company. He suspected they wanted to make sure he didn't tell the prisoners anything he shouldn't. Gray Fawn was there too, keeping to the rear.

Slocum had tried to calm Anderson and Tormey's fears, and seemed to have succeeded. Once he had explained the situation to the survey crew chief and the Irishman, there had been no further argument. Of course, it was obvious even to the thickest of the dozen that argument was point-less, and, if anything, likely to worsen their situation rather than improve it. The most disciplined warriors had been assigned to principal escort duty. They had been warned that they were responsible for the safety of the captives, and that the lives of Sioux women and children were at stake.

Slocum had made it quite clear to Tall Shadow. "Tell your warriors," he'd said, "that if anything happens to any of these men, we will have absolutely no chance whatsoever of carrying out the second half of the plan. And if the plan fails, there will be much blood, more than anyone has ever seen in the Sioux country. Bluecoats will swarm like grasshoppers in the summer fields. They will bring their wagon guns, and they will not stop shooting until every last Sioux man, woman, and child is either dead or in chains."

Tall Shadow had seemed skeptical. "There cannot be so many bluecoats," he said.

Slocum smiled coldly. "I am here to tell you, my friend, that there can be, and there are. You must have heard of the great war between the whites of the north and the whites of the south."

Tall Shadow nodded.

"Well, I was in that war, and I saw it with my own eyes. Armies of one hundred thousand men on each side fighting battles that lasted for three or four days at a time. And when such a battle was finished, there were more dead left in the fields than there are Sioux in all of the Great Plains."

"No, that cannot be."

It was Slocum's turn to nod. "It can be. Someday when this is all behind us, maybe I can take you to the burial ground where you can see with your own eyes—grave after grave after grave after grave, row after row. Men who wore blue coats, and men who wore gray coats. Young men, all dead now, their mothers and fathers still weeping for them after all these winters. It is true, Tall Shadow. I saw it. I *lived* it."

The young Sioux was somber. For a long time he was silent. He kept looking at the prisoners as if trying to imagine a thousand times their number laying dead in the mud.

But he could not imagine such a thing, nor could Slocum explain it to him. It was too alien, and too incredible.

But Tall Shadow believed him somehow, and Slocum knew it.

It was late in the day when they reached the last hill before Black Eagle's small village. The closer they came the more restless the Sioux seemed, as if the urge to explode into vengeful action was getting to be more than they could control. But the painful truth Slocum had revealed had done much to reinforce the determination of the most disciplined warriors. Tall Shadow and Hunts With a Knife had spent much time talking between themselves, glancing now and then at Slocum as if trying once more to determine whether or not he had told the truth. But as Tall Shadow called a halt at the bottom of the last hill, it was clear that they believed him; that they feared for their friends and families, and that they would do as they were told.

Slocum called Gray Fawn and Tall Shadow to one side, dismounted, and asked them to do the same. The warriors massed themselves in a solid wall around the captives.

"We have to go over it one more time," Slocum said.

Tall Shadow nodded.

"Remember," Slocum continued, "no matter what happens, you don't give up the captives. They might try to take me prisoner. They might even shoot me. But that doesn't make any difference, you do exactly what we planned to do. Understand?"

"I understand," Tall Shadow replied.

He turned to Gray Fawn then. "If this doesn't work," he said, "try to get to Colonel Roberts at Fort McAllister. Give him the letter I gave to you. I don't know whether it will make any difference, but it will be your last chance."

Gray Fawn looked frightened. Her lips trembled and her voice shook when she said, "I understand."

He shook Tall Shadow's hand and clapped him on the shoulder. "You take care of her, will you? And don't let her boss you around too much."

Tall Shadow smiled. "I will ask her if it is all right to think for myself once each winter. That is the best I can hope for."

Slocum bent to kiss Gray Fawn on the top of her head, but she tilted her head back and closed her eyes. Slocum glanced at Tall Shadow, who nodded slightly, and then turned away. Wrapping her in his arms, he kissed her on her mouth. The tip of her tongue was like a white-hot blade that probed him deeply, until it took his breath away.

As he let go of her, Slocum said, "Take care of yourself."

"You make it sound as if you will not see me again."

"That may be so," Slocum said.

"I won't allow that," she said, her voice quavering but refusing to break. "I just won't allow it!"

Slocum climbed into the saddle and started toward the hostages. "You men remember that your lives are at stake here," he said. "Do as you've been told, and everything will come out all right."

He was having second thoughts but there was no room for them in his head. He had to be absolutely clear about what was about to happen. He would have to see everything in front of him, possibly make a split-second decision, with dozens, perhaps even hundreds or thousands of lives in the balance.

Shaking his head—as if the distractions could be disposed of so easily—he dug in his heels and rode up the hill. Behind him, he could hear the nickering of the Sioux horses as they followed him. When he reached the top of the hill, he permitted himself one long last look at the men behind him. He thought he spotted Gray Fawn at the back, but he couldn't be sure.

The village looked as he remembered it. A huge fire was already burning in the center of the circle of lodges, a mound of firewood stacked beside it. Several of Crum's troopers were seated beside the flames, tin mess plates in their laps. Farther back, a few small children sat outside the lodges some of which had their sides rolled partway up.

The meadow beyond the village looked strange without the herd of ponies. Its grass had been trampled from both the grazing and the stampede Slocum had engineered.

He looked for Crum, but the lieutenant was nowhere in evidence. He spotted Sergeant Conley standing just outside one of the lodges. Slocum took his time; he knew that the men would sooner or later spot him. He had his Winchester cocked and he cradled it across his saddle.

The big roan seemed restless beneath him, as if the horse was expecting something out of the ordinary. The stallion was loping easily as it neared the bottom of the hill. One of the troopers must have heard him coming, because Slocum saw him stand up and point. The rest of the troopers dropped their plates and went for their guns.

He saw Conley pull a revolver, then run to the pyramid of carbines beside the fire. He grabbed one, and shouted for the rest of the men to get their weapons.

Reining in two hundred yards from the edge of the village, Slocum cupped his hands and shouted, "Lieutenant Crum?"

His voice echoed off the hills surrounding the village, and seemed to come back at him from every direction, as if there were a dozen John Slocums making the same insistent call for the young officer.

But there was no answer.

Once more, he cupped his hands around his mouth and shouted the lieutenant's name. Something stirred in the entrance to one of the lodges. Crum's face, wearing a startled expression, poked into the open. The sun, starting to turn dark orange, gave it a strange, sickly cast.

He watched as Crum came out of the lodge and walked toward the fire. A log cracked, sending a shower of sparks into the air, and the shifting weight ended with a crash. Plumes of dull gray ash rose on the heated air, and caught the darkening sunlight. They seemed to burn without flame or smoke, until they drifted away, and sank out of sight.

"Slocum?" Crum called. "Is that you?"

"It's me," he said, nudging the horse a few paces closer.

"You're in big trouble, boy," Conley barked.

"I'll handle this, Sergeant," Crum snapped, but his voice betrayed his uncertainty. He glared at Conley over his shoulder for a second, then looked back toward Slocum. "You come to surrender, did you, Slocum?"

"Nope. Come to ask *you* to surrender."

Crum looked surprised. "Me? Surrender?"

Slocum eased the roan still closer. He was trying to watch all the troopers at the same time, but they were starting to spread out a little, easing away on either flank. Each had a Sharps repeater clutched in his hand. He'd lost sight of Conley now, and was starting to get worried.

"You heard me, Lieutenant. I want you and your men to put their weapons down and step up to the fire. Do it fast. Do it now!"

"You're in no position to make demands, Slocum. You must be crazy. You're the one who should surrender. You'll be lucky if they don't hang you."

Slocum turned and gave a shrill whistle.

"What the hell are you—" Crum stopped and stepped back. He was staring at the hilltop behind Slocum. His jaw flapped soundlessly, like that of a landed trout.

Slocum watched as Tall Shadow and Hunts With a Knife led the Sioux and the hostages over the hilltop and started down.

"Look closely, Lieutenant. I think you'll see why you should surrender. If you were thinking about reinforcements, forget it."

"This is treason," Crum gasped. He staggered a few steps in a half circle like a man who didn't know which way to run.

"Don't listen to him, Lieutenant," Conley barked. "He won't do anything. We have too many hostages."

Crum turned to look at Conley. He started to speak, then changed his mind. Turning back to Slocum, he said, "Are you telling me that you are holding my men hostage? Is that what you're telling me?"

"That's exactly what I'm telling you."

"What am I supposed to do, give up my weapons with those savages armed to the teeth?"

"Yes sir, that's exactly what you're supposed to do."

"That's . . . that's . . . I can't do. . . ."

"You can and you will, Lieutenant."

"Why are you doing this?"

"Because he's an Injun lover," Conley barked. "Tell him to go to hell! We'll take our chances. We lay down our guns and they'll kill us all."

Crum whirled around again. "Sergeant Conley, I told you to be quiet. I can't think. I have to. . . ." He turned back to Slocum, his face quivering like jelly. He was in a tight spot; tighter than anything he'd ever imagined, and he didn't know where to turn.

"All right," he said. He unbuckled his belt and let his side arm fall to the ground.

"You yellow sonofabitch, Crum!" Conley shouted. He took two quick steps and grabbed a young girl with one thick arm, circling her neck, crouching behind her, a Colt in his hand. The Sharps was in his free hand. "I ain't gonna let you give me up to them redskins!" he shouted.

Crum took a step toward him. Conley's pistol cracked, and Crum staggered backward and sat down with his hands waving in the air in front of his chest. He looked down trying to understand what had just happened to him. Then, as if Slocum held the key, he turned to him. His face was white with shock. "It hurts," he said.

Conley started to back away as the Sioux broke into a gallop, and charged toward the village.

"Lay down your guns, now!" Slocum shouted.

The Sioux were getting closer and closer. Conley dragged the girl behind a lodge and disappeared. Slocum pushed the roan forward, and the troopers dropped their rifles and raised their hands in the air as they backed up.

"Stay where you are," Slocum barked. "They won't hurt you."

Tall Shadow and Hunts With a Knife led two small groups of warriors to each side of the village. They encircled the unarmed troopers and then dismounted. Slocum charged ahead, kicking the roan into a leap over the roaring fire, and on through the village.

"Conley!" he called, dismounting. "Give it up!"

"Go to hell!" Conley shouted.

Tall Shadow sprinted around the far side of the lodges, and Slocum saw him out of the corner of his eye as he moved in behind Conley. "It's over, Sergeant. Let the girl go. Throw down your gun."

"No way in hell, Slocum. No way in hell."

The girl had started to squirm, and Conley was having a tough time holding on to her. He fired at Slocum, but his aim was unsteady, and the bullet sailed harmlessly past him. Slocum couldn't shoot back for fear of hitting the girl.

"Conley," Slocum said, crouching and keeping his eye on the pistol, "you can't get away. There's no need for more bloodshed."

Conley laughed. "You forget one thing, Slocum. I just shot that asshole Crum. I got nothing to lose."

Slocum was watching Tall Shadow out of the corner of his eye, trying to see what the Sioux was planning without giving him away. "You know, Conley, you don't have to—"

"I don't want to hear anymore crap from you, Slocum! I'm sick of this shit, sick of eating lousy food, taking orders from fools like Crum, rotting away out here, just waiting for some damn redskin to take my scalp. I'd just as soon—"

Tall Shadow charged, and Conley must have heard something. He spun around, losing his grip on the girl, who dragged the Sharps with her as she ran, pulling Conley off balance. The sergeant brought his pistol up and fired. The bullet caught Tall Shadow on the fleshy part of his arm and sent him reeling backward.

"Conley!"

The sergeant fell to one knee and turned as Slocum raced toward him. Slocum saw the pistol swinging around and drew his Colt. Conley smiled as the gun in his hand came around. There was no choice. Slocum squeezed the trigger.

Conley fell backward, his gun going off involuntarily before falling from his clenched fingers. A bright smear of blood stained his blue coat just over his heart. As Slocum knelt beside him, the bloodstain glistened in the orange light of the sun for a moment, until his shadow fell over Conley's chest.

The sergeant grinned crookedly. "You done me a favor, Slocum. I was dying to get out of this chicken outfit."

He fell back with a groan. His chest bubbled once, then there was silence. Slocum leaned over Conley, reached out with one hand and, using his thumb, closed the sergeant's staring eyes.

EPILOGUE

Colonel Wesley Roberts drummed his fingers on his huge wooden desk. He had listened quietly, nodding once in a while, and occasionally making notes with a pen that scratched loudly on the paper in front of him. When Slocum was done speaking, Roberts leaned back in his chair, running a hand over his salt-and-pepper beard and sucking on his teeth.

"And you mean to tell me that all of this happened because two damned fools decided to shoot an old man who was trying to ask them for help?"

"Yes sir. You heard what Gray Fawn said, and. . . ."

"Yes, I heard what she said." Roberts looked at her then. "Young lady, I guess the first thing I ought to do is extend my personal regrets for the murder of your grandfather. That never should have happened, and I am deeply sorry."

Gray Fawn nodded, but said nothing.

Warren Anderson cleared his throat. "Colonel, needless to say, I would like to suggest that no action be taken against any of the Sioux involved in the events we've been discussing here. In fact, if anything, I suppose we owe them an apology."

"I wouldn't argue with that, Mr. Anderson," the colonel said. "I don't think Lieutenant Crum would, either. He's lucky to be alive, a bit of a fool, but lucky all the same. I expect he'll be sent back east somewhere, where he can't cause as much trouble. I thought about a court martial, but decided that the sooner this mess is laid to rest, the better for all concerned."

"What about Tall Shadow, Colonel?" Slocum asked.

"Well, he's a strong young man. The post surgeon, Major Meriwether, tells me that he lost a good deal of blood, but he should be fine with some rest." Looking at Gray Fawn, he continued. "You have a remarkable family, young lady. I don't suppose you know that I've met your father. It was at Fort Laramie some time ago, when I had darker hair and a smaller stomach, but I suppose he might remember me. I'd like to see him again. Give him my best regards and ask him if he would like to go hunting sometime, to let me know."

Gray Fawn smiled. "I'll ask him."

Roberts turned back to Slocum. "You took quite a risk, Mr. Slocum. I suppose we all owe you a vote of thanks."

"No thanks necessary, Colonel. I'm just glad it all worked out for the best."

"Would you ever consider a commission in the Yankee army?"

"Not likely, Colonel."

"You change your mind, I'd be happy to use my influence. What do you plan to do now?"

"Well, I think I'd like to wait around until Tall Shadow is well enough to travel, then I'll take him home. I'd like to get to know him a little better. That is, if Mr. Anderson will let me have the time off."

Anderson laughed. "I think I can justify that. And it seems to me like this young lady here deserves a little of your time, too, John."

Slocum blushed.

SPECIAL PREVIEW!

*At the heart of a great nation
lay the proud spirit of the railroads . . .*

RAILS WEST!

The magnificent epic series of the brave pioneers
who built a railroad, a nation, and a dream.

*Here is a special excerpt from this unforgettable saga
by Franklin Carter—available from Jove Books . . .*

Omaha, Nebraska, Early Spring, 1866

Construction Engineer Glenn Gilchrist stood on the melting surface of the frozen Missouri River with his heart hammering his rib cage. Poised before him on the eastern bank of the river was the last Union Pacific supply train asked to make this dangerous river crossing before the ice broke to flood south. The temperatures had soared as an early chinook had swept across the northern plains and now the river's ice was sweating like a fat man in July. A lake of melted ice was growing deeper by the hour and there was still this last critical supply train to bring across.

"This is madness!" Glenn whispered even as the waiting locomotive puffed and banged with impatience while huge crowds from Omaha and Council Bluffs stomped their slushy shorelines to keep their feet warm. Fresh out of the Harvard School of Engineering, Glenn had measured and remeasured the depth and stress-carrying load of the rapidly melting river yet still could not be certain if it would support the tremendous weight of this last supply train. But Union Pacific's vice president, Thomas Durant, had given the bold order that it was to cross, and there were enough fools to be found willing to man the train and its supply cars, so here Glenn was, standing in the middle of the Missouri and about half sure he was about to enter a watery grave.

Suddenly, the locomotive engineer blasted his steam whistle and leaned out his window. "We got a full head of steam and the temperature is risin', Mr. Gilchrist!"

Glenn did not hear the man because he was imagining what would happen the moment the ice broke through. Good Lord, they could all plunge to the bottom of Big Muddy and be swept along under the ice for hundreds of miles to a frozen death. A vision flashed before Glenn's eyes of an immense ragged hole in the ice fed by two sets of rails feeding into the cold darkness of the Missouri River.

The steam whistle blasted again. Glenn took a deep breath, raised his hand, and then chopped it down as if he were swinging an ax. Cheers erupted from both riverbanks and the locomotive jerked tons of rails, wooden ties, and track-laying hardware into motion.

Glenn swore he could feel the weakening ice heave and buckle the exact instant the Manchester locomotive's thirty tons crunched its terrible weight onto the river's surface. Glenn drew in a sharp breath. His eyes squinted into the blinding glare of ice and water as the railroad tracks swam toward the advancing locomotive through melting water. The sun bathed the rippling surface of the Missouri River in a shimmering brilliance. The engineer began to blast his steam whistle and the crowds roared at each other across the frozen expanse. Glenn finally expelled a deep breath, then started to backpedal as he motioned the locomotive forward into railroading history.

Engineer Bill Donovan was grinning like a fool and kept yanking on the whistle cord, egging on the cheering crowds.

"Slow down!" Glenn shouted at the engineer, barely able to hear his own voice as the steam whistle continued its infernal shriek.

But Donovan wasn't about to slow down. His unholy grin was as hard as the screeching iron horse he rode and Glenn could hear Donovan shouting to his fireman to shovel faster. Donovan was pushing him, driving the locomotive ahead as if he were intent on forcing Glenn aside and charging across the river to the other side.

"Slow down!" Glenn shouted, backpedaling furiously.

But Donovan wouldn't pull back on his throttle, which left Glenn with just two poor choices. He could either leap aside and let the supply train rush past, or he could try to swing on board and wrestle its control from Donovan. It might be the only thing that would keep the ice from swallowing them alive.

Glenn chose the latter. He stepped from between the shivering rails, and when Donovan and his damned locomotive charged past drenching him in a bone-chilling sheet of ice water, Glenn lunged for the platform railing between the cab and the coal tender. The locomotive's momentum catapulted him upward to sprawl between the locomotive and tender.

"Dammit!" he shouted, clambering to his feet. "The ice isn't thick enough to take both the weight and a pounding! You were supposed to . . ."

Glenn's words died in his throat an instant later when the ice cracked like rifle fire and thin, ragged schisms fanned out from both sides of the tracks. At the same time, the rails and the ties they rested upon rolled as if supported by the storm-tossed North Atlantic.

"Jesus Christ!" Donovan shouted, his face draining of color and leaving him ashen. "We're going under!"

"Throttle down!" Glenn yelled as he jumped for the brake.

The locomotive's sudden deceleration threw them both hard against the firebox, searing flesh. The fireman's shovel clattered on the deck as his face corroded with terror and the ice splintered outward from them with dark tentacles.

"Steady!" Glenn ordered, grabbing the young man's arm because he was sure the kid was about to jump from the coal tender. "Steady now!"

The next few minutes were an eternity but the ice held as they crossed the center of the Missouri and rolled slowly toward the Nebraska shore.

"Come on!" a man shouted from Omaha. "Come on!"

Other watchers echoed the cry as the spectators began to take heart.

"We're going to make it, sir!" Donovan breathed, banging Glenn on the shoulder. "Mr. Gilchrist, we're by Gawd goin' to make it!"

"Maybe. But if the ice breaks behind us, the supply cars will drag us into the river. If that happens, we jump and take our chances."

"Yes, sir!" the big Irishman shouted, his square jaw bumping rapidly up and down.

Donovan reeked of whiskey and his eyes were bright and glassy. Glenn turned to look at the young fireman. "Mr. Chandlis, have you been drinking too?"

"Not a drop, sir." Young Sean Chandlis pointed to shore and cried, "Look, Mr. Gilchrist, we've made it!"

Glenn felt the locomotive bump onto the tracks resting on the solid Nebraska riverbank. Engineer Donovan blasted his steam whistle and nudged the locomotive's throttle causing the big drivers to spin a little as they surged up the riverbank. Those same sixty-inch driving wheels propelled the supply cars into Omaha where they were enfolded by the jubilant crowd.

The scene was one of pandemonium as Donovan kept yanking on his steam whistle and inciting the crowd. Photographers crowded around the locomotive taking pictures.

"Come on and smile!" Donovan shouted in Glenn's ear. "We're heroes!"

Glenn didn't feel like smiling. His knees wanted to buckle from the sheer relief of having this craziness behind him. He wanted to smash Donovan's grinning face for starting across the river too fast and for drinking on duty. But the photographers kept taking pictures and all that Glenn did was to bat Donovan's hand away from the infernal steam whistle before it drove him mad.

God, the warm, fresh chinook winds felt fine on his cheeks and it was good to be still alive. Glenn waved to the crowd and his eyes lifted back to the river that he knew would soon be breaking up if this warm weather held. He turned back to gaze westward and up to the city of Omaha. Omaha—when he'd arrived last fall, it had still been little more than a tiny riverfront settlement. Today, it could boast a population of more than six thousand, all anxiously waiting to follow the Union Pacific rails west.

"We did it!" Donovan shouted at the crowd as he raised his fists in victory. "We did it!"

Glenn saw a tall beauty with reddish hair pushing forward through the crowd, struggling mightily to reach the supply train. "Who is that?"

Donovan followed his eyes. "Why, that's Mrs. Megan Gallagher. Ain't she and her sister somethin', though!"

Glenn had not even noticed the smaller woman with two freckled children in tow who was also waving to the train and trying to follow her sister to its side. Glenn's brow furrowed. "Are their husbands on this supply train?"

Donovan's wide grin dissolved. "Well, Mr. Gilchrist, I know you told everyone that only single men could take this last one across, but . . ."

Glenn clenched his fists in surprise and anger. "Donovan, don't you understand that the Union Pacific made it clear that there was to be no drinking and no married men on this last run! Dammit, you broke both rules! I've got no choice but to fire all three of you."

"But, sir!"

Glenn felt sick at heart but also betrayed. Bill "Wild Man" Donovan was probably the best engineer on the payroll, but he'd proved he was also an irresponsible fool, one who played to the crowd and was more than willing to take chances with other men's lives and the Union Pacific's rolling stock and precious construction supplies.

"I'm sorry, Donovan. Collect your pay from the paymaster before quitting time," Glenn said, swinging down from the cab into the pressing crowd. Standing six feet three inches, Glenn was tall enough to look over the sea of humanity and note that Megan Gallagher and her sister were embracing their triumphant husbands. It made Glenn feel even worse to think that those two men would be without jobs before this day was ended.

Men pounded Glenn on the back in congratulations but he paid them no mind as he pushed through the crowd, moving off toward the levee where these last few vital tons of rails, ties, and other hardware were being stored until the real work of building a railroad finally started.

"Hey!" Donovan shouted, overtaking Glenn and pulling him up short. "You can't fire me! I'm the best damned engineer you've got!"

"*Were* the best," Glenn said, tearing his arm free. "Now step aside."

But Donovan didn't budge. The crowd pushed around the two large men, clearly puzzled as to the matter of this dispute in the wake of such a bold and daring success only moments earlier.

"What'd he do wrong?" a man dressed in a tailored suit asked in a belligerent voice. "By God, Bill Donovan brought that train across the river and that makes him a hero in my book!"

This assessment was loudly applauded by others. Glenn could feel resentment building against him as the news of his decision to fire three of the crew swept through the crowd. "This is a company matter. I don't make the rules, I just make sure that they are followed."

Donovan chose to appeal to the crowd. "Now you hear that, folks. Mr. Gilchrist is going to fire three good men without so much as a word of thanks. And that's what the working man gets from this railroad for risking his life!"

"Drop it," Glenn told the big Irishman. "There's nothing left to be gained from this."

"Isn't there?"

"No."

"You're making a mistake," Donovan said, playing to the crowd. The confident Irishman thrust his hand out with a grin. "So why don't we let bygones be bygones and go have a couple of drinks to celebrate? Gallagher and Fox are two of the best men on the payroll. They deserve a second chance. Think about the fact they got wives and children."

Glenn shifted uneasily. "I'll talk to Fox and Gallagher but you were in charge and I hold you responsible."

"Hell, we made it in grand style, didn't we!"

"Barely," Glenn said, "and you needlessly jeopardized the crew and the company's assets, that's why you're still fired."

Donovan flushed with anger. "You're a hard, unforgiving man, Gilchrist."

"And you are a fool when you drink whiskey. Later, I'll hear Fox's and Gallagher's excuses."

"They drew lots for a cash bonus ride across that damned melting river!" Donovan swore, his voice hardening. "Gallagher and Fox needed the money!"

"The Union Pacific didn't offer any bonus! It was your job to ask for volunteers and choose the best to step forward."

Donovan shrugged. He had a lantern jaw, and heavy, fist-scarred brows overhanging a pair of now very angry and bloodshot eyes. "The boys each pitched in a couple dollars into a pot. I'll admit it was my idea. But the winners stood to earn fifty dollars each when we crossed."

"To leave wives and children without support?" Glenn snapped. "That's a damned slim legacy."

"These are damned slim times," Donovan said. "The idea was, if we drowned, the money would be used for the biggest funeral and wake Omaha will ever see. And if we made it . . . well, you saw the crowd."

"Yeah," Glenn said. "If you won, you'd flood the saloons and drink it up so either way all the money would go for whiskey."

"Some to the wives and children," Donovan said quietly.

"Like hell."

Glenn started to turn and leave the man but Donovan's voice stopped him cold. "If you turn away, I'll drop you," the Irishman warned in a soft, all the more threatening voice.

"That would be a real mistake," Glenn said.

Although several inches taller than the engineer, Glenn had no illusions as to matching the Irishman's strength or fighting ability. Donovan was built like a tree stump and was reputed to be one of the most vicious brawlers in Omaha. If Glenn had any advantage, it was that he had been on Harvard's collegiate boxing club and gained some recognition for quickness and a devastating left hook that had surprised and then floored many an opponent.

"Come on, sir," Donovan said with a friendly wink as he reached into his coat pocket and dragged out a pint of whiskey. The engineer uncorked and extended it toward Glenn. "So I got a little carried away out there. No harm, was there?"

"I'm sorry," Glenn said, pivoting around on his heel and starting off toward the levee to oversee the stockpiling and handling of this last vital shipment.

This time when Donovan's powerful fingers dug into Glenn's shoulder to spin him around, Glenn dropped into a slight crouch, whirled, and drove his left hook upward with every ounce of power he could muster. The punch caught Donovan in the gut. The big Irishman's cheeks blew out and his eyes bugged. Glenn pounded him again in the solar plexus and Donovan staggered, his face turning fish-belly white. Glenn rocked back and threw a textbook combination of punches to the bigger man's face that split Donovan's cheek to the bone and dropped him to his knees.

"You'd better finish me!" Donovan gasped. " 'Cause I swear to settle this score!"

Glenn did not take the man's threat lightly. He cocked back his fist but he couldn't deliver the knockout blow, not while the engineer was gasping in agony. "Stay away from me," Glenn warned before he hurried away.

He felt physically and emotionally drained by the perilous river crossing and his fight with Donovan. He had been extremely fortunate to survive both confrontations. It had reinforced the idea in his mind that he was not seasoned enough to be making such critical decisions. It wasn't that he didn't welcome responsibility, for he did. But not so much and not so soon.

The trouble was that the fledgling Union Pacific itself was in over its head. No one knew from one day to the next whether it would still be in operation or who was actually in charge. From inception, Vice President Thomas Durant, a medical doctor turned railroad entrepreneur, was the driving force behind getting the United States Congress to pass two Pacific Railway Acts through Congress. With the Civil War just ending and the nation still numb from the shock of losing President Abraham Lincoln, the long discussed hope of constructing a transcontinental railroad was facing tough sledding. Durant himself was sort of an enigma, a schemer and dreamer whom some claimed was a charlatan while others thought he possessed a brilliant organizational mind.

Glenn didn't know what to think of Durant. It had been through him that he'd landed this job fresh out of engineering school as his reward for being his class valedictorian. So far, Glenn's Omaha experience had been nothing short of chaotic. Lacking sufficient funds and with the mercurial Durant dashing back and forth to Washington, there had been a clear lack of order and leadership. It had been almost three years since Congress had agreed to pay both the Union Pacific and the Central Pacific Railroads the sums of $16,000 per mile for track laid over the plains, $32,000 a mile through the arid wastes of the Great Basin, and a whopping $48,000 per mile for track laid over the Rocky and the Sierra Nevada mountain ranges.

Now, with the approach of spring, the stage had been set to finally begin the transcontinental race. One hundred miles of roadbed had been graded westward from Omaha and almost forty miles of temporary track had been laid.

For two years, big paddlewheel steamboats had been carrying mountains of supplies up the Missouri River. There were three entire locomotives still packed in shipping crates resting on the levee while two more stood assembled beside the Union Pacific's massive new brick roundhouse with its ten locomotive repair pits. Dozens of hastily constructed shops and offices surrounded the new freight and switching yards.

There was still more work than men and that was a blessing for veterans in the aftermath of the Civil War joblessness and destruction. Every day, dozens more ex-soldiers and fortune seekers crossed the Missouri River into Omaha and signed on with the Union Pacific Railroad. Half a nation away, the Central Pacific Railroad was already attacking the Sierra Nevada Mountains but Glenn had heard that they were not so fortunate in hiring men because of the stiff competition from the rich gold and silver mines on the Comstock Lode.

Glenn decided he would have a few drinks along with some of the other officers of the railroad, then retire early. He was dog-tired and the strain of these last few days of worrying about the stress-carrying capacity of the melting ice had enervated him to the point of bone weariness.

Glenn realized he would be more than glad when the generals finally arrived to take command of the Union Pacific. He would be even happier when the race west finally began in dead earnest.

A special offer for people who enjoy reading the best Westerns published today.

WESTERNS!

NO OBLIGATION

Mail the coupon below

To start your subscription and receive 2 FREE WESTERNS, fill out the coupon below and mail it today. We'll send your first shipment which includes 2 FREE BOOKS as soon as we receive it.